HEIR TO A DARK INHERITANCE

HEIR TO A DARK INHERITANCE

BY

MAISEY YATES

First published in Great Britain 2013
by Mills & Boon, an imprint of Harlequin (UK) Limited.
Large Print edition 2013
Harlequin (UK) Limited, Eton House,
18-24 Paradise Road, Richmond, Surrey TW9 1SR

© Maisey Yates 2013

ISBN: 978 0 263 23221 9

Harlequin (UK) policy is to use papers that are natural,
renewable and recyclable products and made from
wood grown in sustainable forests. The logging and
manufacturing process conform to the legal environmental
regulations of the country of origin.

Printed and bound in Great Britain
by CPI Antony Rowe, Chippenham, Wiltshire

To Jackie Ashenden,
my writing lifeline and lover of my dark heroes.
Thank you for always encouraging me.

PROLOGUE

ALIK VASIN DOWNED the last of the vodka in his glass and waited for the buzz to make it to his brain. Nothing. It was going to take a lot more alcohol tonight. To have some fun. To feel something.

Either that, or it was going to take a woman. And since that was next on his agenda, he figured he might as well skip the alcohol.

Alik pushed away from the bar and wove through the crush of bodies on the dance floor. The music was so loud there, the bass so heavy he could feel it in his blood. There would be no way to have a conversation with anyone in here. Which was fine by him. He wasn't looking for a talk.

It didn't take long for him to spot a woman who wasn't looking to talk, either.

He approached the blonde skirting the edges of the dance floor. She smiled. Ah yes, he'd found the evening's entertainment. No doubt about it.

He moved closer and she extended her hand, her fingers brushing his chest. Forward. He liked that.

She might even be the kind who wouldn't want to wait to get to the hotel room.

His pocket buzzed and he reached inside and wrapped his hand around his phone. In his experience, women didn't like being thrown over for a phone call, but if his checking it chased her off, another one would come along in just a few moments. If he didn't want to go to bed alone tonight, he wouldn't.

He took the phone from his pocket and saw a number he didn't recognize. Anyone who managed to contact him from a number he didn't know was important.

He held his finger up, an indicator he wanted the woman to wait. She might. She might not. He didn't really care.

He answered the call just before pushing the door open and put the phone up to his ear as he stepped out onto a crowded street in downtown Brussels. A group of women walked by and offered him inviting looks. He might keep an eye out for which club they went to, rather than going back to the blonde waiting for him inside.

He put the phone up to his ear. "Vasin."

And suddenly the cobblestones didn't feel so steady under his feet. He had to wonder if the vodka had finally started working. If it was the cause of the buildings appearing to close in around him. Of the tightness in his chest. If it was making him hear things. If he was imagining what the woman on the other end of the line was saying.

But no. He wasn't. Yes, he was Alik Vasin. Yes, he had been in that region of the United States more than a year earlier.

He stood still for a moment, waited for the earth to right itself beneath his feet. Everything fell away in pieces. The clubs. The women. And he could no longer remember why he was there, on a dark street in Brussels.

There was only the phone call.

Adrenaline shot through his veins. The jolt he'd been missing all night. He would not freeze up. He was not that kind of man. He acted.

Alik hung up and stuffed his hands in his pockets, walking quickly away from the club, his steps heavy and loud on the cobblestone. He had to get to the airport. Had to get to a lab so he could get confirmation.

He took his phone out of his pocket, searching for Sayid's number. His friend would know what to say. Would know what to tell him.

Because it wasn't the vodka. It was just the truth. He knew it, deep in his bones.

He was a father.

CHAPTER ONE

"Did you really think you could keep my child from me?"

Jada stopped on the courthouse steps, the hair on her arms standing on end, the back of her neck prickling with cold sweat. It was the voice of her most dreaded nightmare. A voice she'd never heard before outside of her dreams, and yet she knew that it was him.

Alik Vasin.

A stranger. The man with the power to come in and rip the beating heart from her chest if he chose to do so. The man with the power to devastate her life.

The father of her daughter.

"I don't know what you're talking about," Jada said, inching up the stairs that led to the courthouse. But she knew. She absolutely knew, and apparently he did, too.

"You had the court date changed."

"I had to change it," she said, defiant, confident

in her lie. It didn't feel wrong, or even like a lie, not when she'd told it to protect her child. Jada had spent her life behaving, following the rules, but there were no rules for this situation. There was no right, no wrong. There was only need. The need to keep Leena with her.

"And you thought that since I had to travel halfway around the world on short notice, I would be forced to miss it. Too bad for you I have a private jet."

He didn't look like the kind of man who owned a private jet. He didn't look like a man ready for a court hearing. He was wearing low-slung jeans, held onto his lean hips with a thick belt. He had a rumpled button-up shirt on that somehow looked all the better for being wrinkled, the sleeves pushed up past his elbows, revealing muscular forearms. And aviator sunglasses. Like he was some sort of rock star or something.

He turned his hand and adjusted the buckle on his watch, revealing a dark tattoo, an anchor, on the underside of his wrist. She wondered, briefly, how much something like that had hurt. She wondered what it said about him. He was danger personified, and just looking at him made a shiver course through her body.

On the plus side, his blatant lack of regard for convention made her feel more and more confident about her chances. She'd had Leena in her custody for a year, after all. And this man, her father, had no claim on her beyond the genetic.

Blood was certainly thicker than water, but dirty diapers trumped blood. And she had changed more than her share of those over the past year.

He looked at his watch. "Looks like I've made it with time to spare. I'll be back in a moment."

"Don't rush," Jada said. She took a seat in one of the chairs that lined the door outside of the family courtroom. She wished she could hold Leena right now, but Leena was with the social worker. Jada's arms felt empty. She picked her purse up from the floor, her phone out of one of the pockets, opened an app and played it mindlessly. She just needed to keep her hands busy. And her mind vacant.

"Good. I didn't miss anything."

She looked up and a swear word rushed out of her mouth. He looked…it wasn't fair how he looked. He was in a black suit, open at the collar, everything fitted perfectly to his well-muscled physique. The dark fabric poured over him like liquid, flowing with his movements, revealing strength, power. He looked like the sort of man who got what he wanted with the snap of a finger. The kind of man who had women falling at his feet with a glance.

He'd gone from rumpled traveler to James Flipping Bond in ten seconds flat.

Although, Bond was always fighting the Russians, so maybe he was more of a Bond villain.

"I see you decided to dress for the occasion," she said.

He'd removed the sunglasses, and for the first time she could see his eyes. They were somewhere between blue and gray, like the sea during a storm.

"It seemed the thing to do," he said, his lips quirking up into a smile. He seemed entirely unruffled, as if the outcome of this didn't matter to him at all. It meant everything to her. This, Leena, was her entire life. All she had left.

"It seemed the thing to do? Well, I suppose it's good that going out for Chinese food didn't seem the thing to do at the moment instead. Is that all she is to you? Just…is this just an experiment for you? Why did you even bother to show up?"

"She's my daughter," he said, his tone betraying no emotion, no concern. Just stating a fact. "That means I must claim responsibility for her."

"Responsibility? Is that what she is to you?"

She caught a hint of steel in his eyes. "She's my blood. Not yours."

Jada snorted and crossed her arms beneath her breasts. "I've only raised her from the time she was born. What do I matter?" She didn't know where this strength was coming from. She only knew she had it, and she had to use it. There was no one standing behind her. No one on her side. No one but herself.

"I didn't know about her," he said.

"Because her mother thought you were dead. And why did she think that? Did you tell her you were going off on some secret mission? That's the sort of thing a man like you might say to get a woman into bed."

"If I told her that, it was true," he said.

She blinked. "If? You don't remember?"

He shrugged. "Not specifically."

And then her brain caught up with the rest of his claim. "And you *were* on a mission of some kind?"

"How old is the child?"

Jada blinked. "You don't know?"

"I know nothing about this," he said. "I got a phone call while I was in Brussels, telling me that if I didn't come and claim a child I didn't know I had by a certain date, I would lose my rights to her forever. Then I went and got testing done to confirm that I am in fact the father, and I am, just so you know. Then yesterday I got a letter saying my parental rights would be terminated and she would be adopted to someone else if I failed to come to a hearing that had been moved to today."

"She's one. She just had her birthday." Just the two of them in Jada's little house, on the same street where she'd lived for eight years. "Where were you a little over a year and a half ago?"

His mouth twitched. "Near here. I was in Portland seeing to some business."

She put her hands on her hips. "Ah. Business."

"I can't talk about the exact nature of it."

Disgust filled her. He was the sort of man she'd been blessed never to have had any interaction with. She'd married too young and her husband had been completely decent. She didn't think men like this, men who bed-hopped with zero discrimination, were real outside of terrible movies. "I can guess. I've been caring for the results of that *business*."

One brow shot upward. "Just an added bonus to my trip. I'm not a sex tourist."

Jada blinked, heat rushing into her cheeks. "You are direct, aren't you?"

"And you are prickly. And extremely judgmental."

And not accustomed to people who were so comfortable talking about their bad behavior. He seemed to wear it like a badge of honor. "You're here to take my child from me—what reaction did you want me to have to you?"

He looked at their surroundings. They were the only two people in the antechamber. "I didn't anticipate being stuck in the lobby with you, I have to say."

"And yet you are. Answer me this…what does a man who travels the world, doing Lord knows what, want with a baby? Do you have a wife?" She hoped not, all things considered.

"No."

"Other children?"

"Not as far as I know," he said, a smile that could only be described as naughty curving his lips. "Clearly these things can surprise you."

"Not most people, Mr. Vasin," she bit out. "So, why do you want her?"

It was a good question. One Alik didn't know the answer to. All he knew was that if he turned and walked away, if he never met her, never made sure she was cared for, if he left her to fight her way through life as he'd had to do, then there would officially be no hell hot enough for him.

Forgetting about the phone call had crossed his mind. Not making it to the hearing had crossed his mind. But with each thought had come a twinge in his chest, a brand on a conscience he hadn't known he'd possessed.

He didn't particularly want her. But no matter what, he found he couldn't leave, either.

He gave the only answer he had. "Because she is mine."

"Hardly a good reason."

"Why do *you* want her so badly, Ms. Patel?" he asked, returning her formality. "She is not your child, no matter how you feel."

"Is that so? Blood relation, even to a stranger, is more important than the care that's been given? Is that how you see it?"

Alik looked down at the woman in front of him, all fire and passion. Beautiful, and if it was any other situation, his thoughts might have turned to seduction. Black, glossy hair, golden skin and honey-colored eyes, combined with a petite and perfect figure, made her a very tempting package.

Though, at the moment she was also a dangerous one. She was tiny, barely reaching the middle of his chest and yet she did not fear him. She seemed ready to physically attack him if need be.

Not in the way he would like, he imagined.

"It is not an emotional matter," he said. "It is black-and-white in my eyes. I am her father. You are not her mother."

She drew back, a cobra preparing to strike. "How dare you?"

"Mr. Vasin? Ms. Patel?" A small woman in a black jacket and slacks opened the door and poked her head out. "We're ready for you both."

As Mr. Vasin is here and clearly of sound mind, and, having submitted to a paternity test, has proven to be the father, we have no reason not to release his child into his custody.

Jada replayed the last ten minutes of the hearing in her mind, over and over again. The judge was sorry, the caseworkers regretful. But there was simply no reason why Leena shouldn't be with her father. Her *billionaire* father, as it turned out, which she knew had bearing on the ruling regardless of what anyone said.

How could it not? Jada was a housewife with no spouse to support her. Her only source of income came from her late husband's life insurance settlement and as generous as it was, it wasn't a billion dollars.

That, combined with the irrefutable proof of his paternity, when it was made clear that he had been wronged, the victim of a misunderstanding, had meant Jada hadn't had a case. Not in anyone else's mind. In hers, she had the only case that mattered. But no one else cared.

And now, Leena was with this Alik Vasin, in a private room so the two of them could get to know each other. Have an introduction. They couldn't let Jada take Leena with her. She was a flight risk. Another thing everyone was very regretful about.

Jada leaned against the wall in the empty hallway and gasped for breath. No matter how much air she took in she was still suffocating. Her chest was locked tight, and she tried to breathe in, but her lungs wouldn't expand. She wondered if her heart had stopped beating, too.

Her knees shook, gave way, and she slid down the wall, sitting with her legs drawn up to her chest, not caring that she was in a skirt, not caring if anyone saw. She hated that this feeling was so familiar. That it slipped back on as easy as an old pair of jeans. Shock. Grief. Loss.

Losing Sunil had been hard enough. Unfair. Unexpected. No one planned to be a widow at twenty-five. Coming to terms with it, with being alone, when she'd leaned on her parents, and then her husband, for all of her life, had been the hardest thing she'd ever gone through. She was still going through it.

Losing Leena on top of it…it wasn't fair. How much was one person expected to lose? How long before she was simply gutted, left empty, with nothing and no one to care for her? No one to care for. And then what was she supposed to do with herself?

Her shoulders shook and a sob worked its way up her throat, her body shuddering with the force of it. People were walking by, trying not to stare at her as she dissolved, utterly and completely, in the hall of the courthouse.

And she didn't care. What did it matter if a bunch of strangers thought she was losing her mind? She might very well be. And if they felt uncomfortable being in the presence of her grief, she didn't care. It was nothing compared to trying to live inside her body. Nothing compared to contending with the pain she was dealing with.

"Ms. Patel." That voice again.

She looked up from her position on the floor,

and saw the man, the man who had taken her baby from her. There was only one thing that stopped her from going for his throat. Only one thing stopping her from opening her purse, finding her mace and unleashing her fury on those stormy gray eyes.

Leena.

He was holding a squirming Leena in his arms. And she was squirming to try to get to Jada. She could only stare at her daughter for a moment, hungry to take in every detail. To remember every bit of her.

Jada scrambled to her feet and extended her arms. Leena leaned away from Alik's body, and he had no choice but to deposit the fussing, wiggling child into her arms.

Jada clung to her daughter, and Leena clung to her. Jada closed her eyes and pressed her face into her daughter's silky brown hair, inhaled her scent. Lavender shampoo and that sweet, wonderful smell unique to babies.

She didn't feel like she was drowning now. She could breathe again, her heart finding its rhythm.

"Mama!" Leena's exclamation, so filled with joy and relief. And Jada broke to pieces inside.

"It's okay," she whispered, more for her benefit than her daughter's. "It's okay." And she knew she lied. But she needed the lie like air and she wouldn't deny herself.

"She does not like me," Alik said, his voice frayed. For the first time since she'd seen him, he was betraying his own discomfort with the situation.

"You're a stranger," she said.

"I'm her father." He said it as if a one-year-old child cared about genetics.

"She doesn't care if you're related to her or not. Not in the least. I am her mother as far as she's concerned. The only mother she knows."

"We need to talk."

"What about?"

"About this," he said, his voice slightly ragged, a bit of that smooth charm of his finally slipping. "About what we need to do."

She didn't know what he meant, but she knew that right now she was holding Leena, so the rest didn't matter.

"Where?" she asked.

"My car. It is fitted with a car seat."

"Okay," she said. Going with him should feel strange; after all, she didn't know the man. But the court had found no reason he couldn't be a fit father. That meant they were going to send her baby off with this man, by herself. So she was hardly going to hesitate over getting in his car with him, all things considered.

She swallowed hard. There was no one else to do this. She was the final authority here, the only one who could change things. And she would take every second with Leena she could get.

She followed him out of the courthouse and down the steps. He pulled out his phone and spoke into it. She wasn't sure what language he was speaking. It wasn't Russian, English or Hindi, that much she knew. A man of many talents, it seemed.

A moment later a black limousine pulled up against the curb and Alik leaned over, opening the back door. "Why don't you get her settled."

She complied mutely, putting Leena, who was starting to nod off after her traumatic afternoon, into the seat and then climbing in and sitting in the spot next to hers. She hadn't wanted to take any chances that he might drive off while she was rounding the car. Paranoid, maybe, but there was no such thing as too paranoid in a situation like this.

She was momentarily awed by the luxuriousness of the car. She'd ridden in a limo after her wedding, but it hadn't been anywhere near this nice.

The seats lined the interior of the limo, leaving the middle open. There was a cooler with champagne in it.

That made her bristle. Had he been planning on celebrating his victory over champagne? A toast to stealing her child away? She wanted to hit him. To hurt him. Give him a taste of what she was dealing with.

"What is it you wanted to speak to me about?" she asked, her voice sharper than she intended.

He closed the door behind him and settled into place. "Drink?"

"No. No drink. What is it you wanted to talk about?"

"How did you meet the child's mother?"

"Leena," she bit out. "Her name is Leena."

"What sort of name is that?"

"Hindi. She's named for my mother."

"She should have a Russian name. I'm Russian."

"And I'm Indian, and she's my daughter. And really, aren't you some kind of arrogant, thinking you can come and just take my child away from her home, away from her mother and then, on top of it all rename her?"

His dark brows shot upward. "I will not rename her. It is not a bad name."

"Thank you," she said, cursing her own good manners. She shouldn't be thanking him. She should be macing him.

"Now," he said, straightening, his posture stiff, like he was about to start a business meeting, "how did you meet Leena's mother?"

"Just…through an adoption agency. She told me the baby's father was dead and that she couldn't possibly raise the child on her own. It was a semi-open adoption. She was able to choose the person she wanted to take her. It wasn't easy for her." She remembered the way the other woman had looked after giving birth, when she'd handed Leena to Jada. She'd looked so tired. So sad. But also relieved. "But it was right for her."

"And the adoption?"

"Normally they're finalized within six months of placement. In Oregon the birth mother can't sign the papers until after the birth, which makes it all take a bit longer. And we were held up further because…because while she listed the birth father as dead, it wasn't something that was confirmed. She had your name, but there was no record of your death, and neither could you be found to sign away your rights. And it hadn't been long enough for you to simply be declared absentee."

"And then they found me."

"Yes, they did. Lucky me."

"I am sorry for you, Jada. I am." He didn't sound it at all. He sounded like a man doing a decent impression of someone who might be sorry, but he personally didn't sound sorry at all. "But it doesn't change the fact that Leena is my daughter. I can't simply walk away from her."

"Why not? Because you're just overcome by love and a parental bond?" She didn't believe that for a moment.

"No. Because it is the right thing to do to care for your children, your family. Leena is the only family I have."

At another time she might have felt sorry for the man. As it was, she felt nothing.

"Caring for her would mean having her with me," she said.

"I can understand how you might see it that way." He looked out the window. "She does not like me. She cries when I pick her up. And frankly, I don't have the time to be a full-time caregiver to an infant."

"Then why did you come?"

"Because the other alternative was having nothing to do with her, and that was not a possible solution in my mind."

"So what does that mean then? You're just going to hire nannies?"

"That was my thought. I was wondering if you would like to take a position as Leena's nanny."

"You what?"

Jada couldn't believe the man was serious. The nanny? To her own child? An employee of the man who was stealing everything from her?

Leena was her light in the darkness. She was everything to her. Being her mother had become the entirety of Jada's identity. And her daughter had become her whole heart.

And he wanted her to be an employee. One he could fire at a moment's notice. A termination he could delay until a later date. A date he saw fit.

"Did you just ask me to be the nanny to my own daughter?"

"As a court ruling just declared, she is not your daughter."

"If you say that one more time so help me I will—"

"It is up to you. Hang on to your pride if you wish, but I'm offering you a chance to see your daughter. To be a part of her life still."

"How can you do this to me?" she asked, the words scraping her throat raw. Everything in her hurt. Everything. He had come in, taken her newly repaired life and shattered it all around her again, and she didn't know how she would reclaim it. It had taken so long to rebuild, to repurpose, to find out what she would do, who she would be.

She'd loved her husband, but he couldn't give her children. And every time other options came up, he shut down. It was a reminder, he'd told her, of all he could not give her. Of what she would have to get from someone else. No, there would be no artificial insemination. She wouldn't carry another man's baby. Adoption had been something he'd said they'd consider, but he never truly had. All the brochures she brought him, all the links to websites she sent him, went ignored.

When the dust had settled after her husband's death, it had been the thing she'd latched onto. She wasn't a wife anymore, but she could be a mother.

And now he was ripping it from her hands. Leaving her arms empty.

"I'm not doing anything to you. Leena is my child and I am claiming her, as is the responsible and right thing to do."

"You have a warped sense of right, Mr. Vasin."

"Alik," he said. "You can call me Alik. And my sense of right seems to match that of the justice system, so one might argue that it is you with a warped sense of justice."

She blinked. "My sense of justice involves the heart, not just laws written on paper, unconnected to specific people and events."

"And that is where we differ. Nothing I do involves the heart." She looked at his eyes, black, soulless. Except for that moment in the courthouse when he'd been holding Leena. Then there had been emotion. Fear. Uncertainty. A man who clearly knew nothing about children.

And he wanted her to be the nanny. He wanted to assume the position as Leena's father and demote her to staff. This man who had been living his life, a full complete life apart from Leena, now wanted to come and take the heart from her.

"She's all I have," Jada said, her voice trembling, emotion betraying her now "All I have in the world."

"So you say no because of pride?"

"And because I am not my child's nanny! I am her mother. The idea of simply being treated as though I'm paid to be there…" It hit at her very identity, who she was. She had been Sunil's wife, and then she had become Leena's mother. She couldn't be nothing again. Not again.

"I would pay you to be there. I can hardly ask you to forfeit whatever job you might have and come be her nanny for free now, can I?"

"How can you…"

"I will of course allow you to live in whatever house I install her in. It will be simpler that way for all involved. I have a penthouse in Paris and one in Barcelona. A town house in New York, though I suspect you would find it rather too busy…."

"And what about you? Where will you be in all of this?"

He shrugged. "I will go on as I have. But you have no need to worry about Leena. As the judge pointed out when he opened up my file—I am a wealthy man."

"Somehow all of your wealth and power doesn't impress me very much, not when your idea of raising a child is to install her in a house somewhere in the world while you leave her with staff!"

"Not just any staff. You. You would be very well-trusted staff."

"You bastard!" No. She wouldn't do it. She couldn't do it. Couldn't allow this man who didn't even want to live in the same home as his daughter to come in and steal everything she had built for herself. For Leena.

"No," she said, the word broken, just like everything inside of her.

"Excuse me?"

"No. Stop the car."

She didn't know what she was doing. Until the moment the car pulled up to the curb and she looked at Leena, and back at Alik. She thought again of the fear in his eyes as he'd held Leena at the courthouse. Of the way Leena had struggled to escape his arms.

And she knew.

"No." She opened the door to the car. "I am her mother. You can't simply demand a change of job title. If you think you're her father because of a magical blood bond then you go and you take care of her."

Her heart was in her throat, her stomach pitching violently. But it was her hope. Her only hope. And it was all born out of some insane idea that what she'd witnessed in this hard, inscrutable man's eyes was truly fear.

And if she was misreading him, there was every chance she would lose her child forever.

But if you don't, he'll always have the power. He has to know that you're right. That he needs you.

She closed the door to the limo, the gray sky reflected in the tinted windows, obscuring Alik, obscuring Leena, from view. Panic clawed at her, tore her to shreds inside.

She turned away and closed her eyes, trying to breathe. She couldn't. A sob caught in her chest. And then Jada started walking away. And she just prayed that Alik would follow.

CHAPTER TWO

ALIK HAD FACED DOWN terrorists hell-bent on blowing him into pieces and scattering his remains in the ocean. He'd dogged his way across enemy lines, into an enemy camp, to save the life of a friend. He'd spent hours calculating tactical strategies for nations at war, finding the smart way to get in and win the battle.

None of it had shaken him. A welcome burst of adrenaline, the rush of having survived, he got all of that from it. But never fear.

He felt it now. Staring down into the dewy eyes of his child. Her little face crumpled and she let out a wail that filled the inside of the limo.

"Don't go yet," he said to his driver. "Don't go."

Leena cried, louder and louder, and Alik had no idea what he was expected to do. He looked out the window, and he didn't see Jada. She was gone. Somewhere into the shopping center they were near, he imagined, but he didn't know where.

Unless she'd hailed a cab and simply left them both. It didn't seem like something she would do, but he admitted, willingly, he knew nothing about emotion. About mothers who stayed with their children.

Jada wasn't even Leena's mother. But he was her father.

He didn't know how to comfort a child. He didn't have a clue as to how to go about it. No one had held him. No one had sung him songs or rocked him until he stopped crying. It was very possible he had never cried.

Leena on the other hand, did. Quite well.

He had always intended to hire a nanny, and when he'd gone out into the hall he'd felt, for the first time in his memory, like he was in a situation he could not control. And when he had seen Jada slumped against the wall, crying into her hands, he knew he'd found the solution.

But then she'd left. She wanted more, and he had no idea what more it was she wanted.

Alik had given up on emotion long ago. His body had put all of that into a deep freeze, protecting him from the worst of his experiences while growing up. And by the time he hadn't needed the protection anymore, it was far too late for anything to thaw.

He experienced things through the physical. Sex and alcohol, and, in his youth, various other stimulants, had done a good job of providing him with sensation where the frozen organ in his chest simply did not.

It was how things were for him. It was convenient too, because when he had to carry out a mission that was less than savory, whether on the battlefield, as he'd once done, or in the boardroom, as he did now, he simply went to his mind. Logic always won.

And after that, there was always a party to go to. He'd learned how to manufacture happiness from his surroundings. To pull it into the darkness that seemed to dominate his insides and light the way with it, temporarily. A night of dancing, drinking and sex. It created a flash, a spark in the oppressive dark. It burned out as quickly as it ignited, but it was a hell of a lot better than endless blackness.

Except he didn't feel vacant now. He felt panicked, and he found it wasn't an improvement. Without thinking, he undid Leena's seat and pulled her into his lap. She shrieked and jerked away from him, and with that came a punch of something—

emotion, pain—to his chest that nearly knocked him back.

As afraid as he was, she was just as scared. Of him.

"Mama! Mama mama mama." The word, just sounds really, came fast and furious, over and over, intermingled with sobs.

He tried to speak. To say something. But he had no idea what to say. What did you say to a screaming baby? He'd never wanted this. Never imagined it. He truly might have turned away if not for Sayid. If not for the conversation they'd had when he'd left Brussels.

"You have to claim her, Alik. She is your responsibility. You have so many resources at your disposal, so many things you can provide her with. She is your blood, your family."

"I have family without blood," Alik had said, a reference to Sayid's family, to whom he had sworn absolute allegiance.

"A family by choice. She is your family. You are bound to her. To dishonor something so strong would be a mistake."

"No, my only mistake was coming here for the weekend instead of heading down to Paris or Barcelona to get laid."

"Running is your specialty, Alik," Sayid had said, his tone deathly serious. *"But you can't change what is by running. Not this time."*

His friend was right. Alik lived his whole life moving at a dead run. But he was never running *from* something. Nothing scared him that much. But he wasn't really running to something, either. He was simply getting through as quickly, as loudly and recklessly, as possible.

He found it was the loud and reckless things in life that offered the most return in terms of what they made him feel. And he was hungry for feeling. For tastes of what years of existing in survival mode had denied him.

Maybe that, more than Sayid's comments, had been the deciding factor in why he'd come. That or watching the other man's life, watching all of the change it had brought about for Sayid to acquire a wife and children.

Either way, when he'd decided to come after his daughter, he hadn't made the decisions hesitantly or lightly. No, there had been no instant bond between them, but he had hardly expected that. Alik had never bonded to people instantly. Sometimes he simply never did.

Sayid was the exception, and then later, Sayid's

family. But he'd been twenty-eight when he'd met his friend, who was more a brother to him than anything else, and it had been his first experience of caring for another human being.

It still didn't come easily to him. But swearing his allegiance? That came as simply as seeing whose name was on the check. It always had for him. Even now that he'd moved into the business of tactical, cutthroat corporate raider, rather than tactical, cutthroat mercenary and overthrower of governments, that fact remained true.

His loyalty could be bought, and once he was purchased, he would defend those he was loyal to till death if he had to. And then, when the job was done, he would break the bonds as easily as they'd been forged.

Again, Sayid was the exception. A job gone wrong, turned into a rescue mission to save the life of the sheikh, even when everyone else had given up, had made their bond unbreakable.

He would simply choose to cultivate that bond with his child. She had bought his loyalty with her blood, a check that could never simply be cashed, could never just disappear.

That meant, no matter what, he would defend her. Fight for her, die for her.

Or pound the streets as long as it took, looking for the woman she called mama.

"I will protect you," he said to her, looking at her red, tear-streaked face. "That is my promise."

His daughter was unimpressed with the vow.

He pushed the door to the limo open. "Wait here," he said to his driver.

He got out, holding Leena, who was squirming and screeching against his chest. People were staring at him, at them. He was used to being able to fly under the radar when he wanted to. Used to making a scene only when he wanted to. But he had no control over this scene.

How a tiny child could assume total control over things with the ease most people breathed astounded him. He walked down the sidewalk, cursing the rain, and the knots of kids in skinny jeans smoking cigarettes and blocking his way.

Cursing his total lack of control.

There was a clothing store, a pizza place and a coffeehouse along the main drag of the shopping center, and he was willing to bet that Jada hadn't gone far.

He pushed open the door to the coffee place and saw her there, clutching a mug in both of her hands, looking ashen and in shock.

He crossed the coffee shop, wiggling baby attempting to impede his progress, and stopped in front of her table.

"Tell me then, Jada Patel, if you do not take the position as my nanny, what will you do?"

She looked at him, the relief that washed over her so strong it was tangible. And yet she didn't move to take the baby from his arms. Didn't try to relieve him.

She didn't respond. She simply looked at him with eyes that conveyed a depth of emotion he hadn't known was possible to feel.

"You don't seem to have a very strong sense of self-preservation," he said, shifting the baby in his arms. "I have offered you a chance to come and live with my daughter, to continue caring for her. You've as much as admitted that you have nothing here if you don't get to keep her. You have no husband. No girlfriend or other sort of lover, obviously. They would have come to the hearing with you, offered support."

She looked down into her coffee mug. "No. I don't have a husband."

"Then you have nothing to leave behind."

She looked away, her eyes glassy, reflecting the gray sky outside the coffee shop's window. "Leaving here isn't the problem." She looked back at him. "What assurance do I have that you won't simply fire me one day? Cast me out onto the street without any warning some day five years down the road and put me in the position of losing her then? I couldn't bear it. I can't bear it now, so part of me wants to take the chance, but I am giving you all of my power, the power over my life if I take the position, and I don't like it at all."

"I don't blame you. I wouldn't like it, either, and yet I see very little in the way of other options."

Jada fought the panic that was rising inside her. Panicking wasn't going to help. She had to think. Had to figure out what to do.

She wished, so desperately, that there was someone she could ask. Her friends…she could hardly stand to be around them. They just looked at her with sad eyes, touched her like they were afraid she was cracking, breaking like a piece of delicate glass. And they'd all thought her crazy when she'd decided to adopt.

Her parents had been gone for so long now. Her father when she was a teenager, her mother six years after that.

And then there was Sunil. She would have turned to him, would have asked him what to do. After he'd died, she'd felt like she was drifting. Unable to think, unable to make a decision. The only thing that had gotten her out of bed every day was the knowledge that he would have wanted her to. He would have told her that there would be something else for her. Something good. And while he hadn't been enthusiastic about adoption during their marriage, she knew he wouldn't have wanted her to be alone.

The something good she'd been waiting for was Leena. From the moment she'd seen Leena, tiny and pink, swaddled in a blanket with her hospital cap fitted snugly over her mop of brown hair, Jada had known she would give her life for her daughter.

Becoming Leena's nanny wasn't even close to giving up her life. But it wasn't the thought of leaving home that frightened her. She had no home without Leena anyway. It was the fact that, at Alik's pleasure, at his whim, he could still tear her daughter away from her at any moment.

She would have no parental rights. She would be nothing more than hired help, waiting for the ax to fall. Loss, when it came suddenly, was hideous. But living her life knowing that any day could bring it would be unbearable.

"So what you need is more security?" he asked. "Something that would feel legal and permanent?"

"Yes, something that would feel more stable, so that I wasn't wondering if you were simply going to sweep through one day and decide I was no longer needed."

She looked at him, into those stormy gray eyes, and a shiver ran through her body. He had a kind of easy grace, a relaxed posture that made him look like he was at ease with the world, with his surroundings.

But what she saw in his eyes just then proved that he was lying to the world. He was ice beneath the exterior.

"You are the kind of woman," he said, "who would never sell her allegiance." The way he said it, with a mix of wonder and admiration, surprised her. "You remind me of someone I know."

"That's all very well and good, but it doesn't solve my problems."

"And I now live to solve your problems?"

"I think we both can see that no matter how tough you play, you have no idea of what you're doing with a child."

"I can hire someone else."

"And you think that would make her happy? Does she not notice when I'm gone?"

That hit him. Square in the chest. A strong, sudden burning of loss. He'd been two or three when he'd been left at an orphanage in Moscow. He didn't remember his mother's face. Or her voice. Or where he'd lived before then. But he remembered loss. Loss so deep, so confusing and painful.

"She would notice," he said, because there was no lying about that. Something had to be done. He knew now he stood in a terrible position. That of abandoning his child, or tearing his child away from the only woman she'd ever known as her mother.

He was trapped.

"You need to come up with a solution we can both be satisfied with."

Jada didn't know how she'd kept from bursting into tears. She was on the edge of breaking completely. But she had to be strong. She had to show Alik that he wasn't in charge. She had to take back control somehow.

This was her life. The life she was creating for herself, and he didn't get to own it. She'd had enough of being jerked around by fate or whatever it was that had reached down and disordered everything. She was done with that. Done with feeling like a victim. Done with allowing life to make her one.

Alik looked down at Leena, his discomfort obvious, then looked back at Jada.

"What do you need?" he asked, his voice frayed, his expression that of a desperate man.

"I need security," she said. "I need to be her mother, because no matter whether you understand it or not, that's what I am, and that's what a child needs. A mother, not a caregiver, not an absentee father. Someone who is there with her. Always."

He looked at her for a moment, black eyes completely unreadable, his handsome face schooled into a mask. "You think something of permanence would be best for Leena."

"Yes."

He nodded slowly. "I may have a solution to your problems. You don't like the idea of my simply… how did you put it? Dumping my child off somewhere in the world with nothing but staff. You think she should have a family, a real family."

"Everyone should."

"Perhaps, but it is not reality. Still, if I could find a way to make that happen for her…having a family is very important, yes?"

Jada nodded, her throat tightening. "Yes."

"I would hate to deny my child anything of importance."

She wanted to scream at him that he was denying his child her mother, and yet she knew it would do no good. He simply didn't seem to understand the connection she felt for Leena. He didn't seem to understand love. And losing control wouldn't win this battle. When he pushed, she had to push back.

"Perhaps then, I should take a wife," he said.

Pain crashed through her. He still didn't get it.

The thought of another woman filling her position, of another woman being the caregiver for her daughter, made her see red. And she knew that was selfish, and she didn't care.

"That easily?" she asked. "That easily you'll just find a wife? One who will care for Leena like she's her own child?"

"I've already found her," he said, gray eyes fixed on her.

She felt the chill from his eyes seep through her skin, making her tremble. "Have you?" she asked, not sure what he was going to say, only that she wasn't going to like it. Only that it was going to change everything.

"You didn't like my offer of coming to be my nanny. Would you like to be my wife?"

CHAPTER THREE

"Do I want to be your…wife?"

He'd said it so casually, so utterly void of emotion that she was certain she must have misheard him.

"Yes," he said. "As you've made it clear, my offer of nanny is unacceptable. And you are right—without you, the child is unhappy."

"Leena," she bit out again, frustrated by his insistence on detachment.

"I know her name." He bent and handed her Leena, a rush of love washing over her as she felt her daughter's weight in her arms. He started to pace beside the table in front of her. "It's a simple thing, one that will protect both us and my daughter legally. You will be able to adopt her and, should we divorce, which I have no doubt we will, unless we find each other so unobtrusive that the marriage simply never gets in our way, we will be able to work out a shared custody agreement."

"I…it is *possible* for an unmarried couple to

work out an adoption. It's more difficult…there needs to be a clear emotional involvement, but…"

"And why make it more difficult? This will be much more simple. Proving a legal connection is much simpler than faking an emotional one, don't you think?"

Yes, she did think. She was sure he was right. It would protect her. It would make her Leena's mother. It would give her the adoption she wanted. But…but there was this man, this stranger. And he was asking to be her husband.

For the second time in her life, everything had changed in one day. She tried, she tried desperately, not to remember the day three years ago when she'd gotten a call from Sunil's office saying he had been sent to the hospital.

Tried not to remember what it had been like, driving there, feeling shocked, dazed. Then seeing him in the bed. He'd looked so sick. Like he was a man barely clinging to life.

Because that was what he had been. And only a few hours later, he'd lost his grip on it.

And her perfect world had crashed down around her. Three years spent rebuilding, trying to pick up the pieces, and Alik Vasin had come along and broken it all again.

"You can't just get married for those kinds of reasons," she said. Her lips felt cold, her entire face prickly.

"Why not? Can you think of a better reason?"

"Love," she said. It was the craziest thing she'd ever heard. And the worst thing was, she didn't know if she could say no.

She looked at Leena and her heart lodged in her throat. If she said no, would this be the last she saw of her? Would she never see her grow? Hear her speak in sentences? Watch her go from a baby, to a child, to a teenager and finally, a young woman? All of her dreams, ash at her feet. Again.

Unless she said yes. She was the one who had demanded more. And now that she was getting the offer, could she really say no?

He frowned, one shoulder lifting. A casual dismissal. "Marriage has never meant very much to me. Marriage is a legal covenant, and it protects a lot of legal rights. That to me makes legal issues the most logical reason to marry."

"I don't even know you."

"I'm not asking you to know me, I'm asking you to marry me. Then my daughter will have a mother and a father. She will be cared for in every way that counts."

Jada blinked, trying to catch up with Alik's logic. Trying to understand it. He sounded so certain, and he moved so quickly, she could scarcely process one thing he'd said before he'd moved on to something else completely.

"How can you simply suggest something like this so…calmly?"

"Because it doesn't matter to me whether you're my nanny or my wife. Nothing will change, and it will offer you the protection that you desire."

"And why is it so important to you to give me that?"

"Additional stability for my daughter. And…" He hesitated. "Her attachment to you is very strong. She…seems to love you. I would hate to cause her any pain."

The way he said it was odd, as though he didn't truly understand either emotion he spoke about. Like he was trying to say the right things, or forcing himself to think the right things, but wasn't quite managing it.

It was crazy. Totally and completely. But she had nothing left here, not without Leena. No reason not to accept the insane offer.

You don't know him.

No, she didn't know him. But if she didn't go,

her daughter would. Without her there to protect her. No. That couldn't happen. It wouldn't. No matter the cost.

Unbidden, she thought of her own wedding day, more than eight years ago. She'd been so young. So full of hope for the future. And so very much in love.

Marrying Alik, making him her husband, she felt like it made a mockery of that. Felt like she was putting Alik in a place that should be reserved for another man. The man that she'd loved with all of her heart.

Oh, Sunil, please forgive me.

She didn't know if he would have been able to. She wasn't sure if he'd truly understood her desire to have children. If he'd realized how deep it went. Or maybe he had, and he simply couldn't acknowledge it, because for him, it would mean facing how much he'd failed her. But she'd never seen it that way. She would have been happy, even then, to adopt.

Still, just for a moment, she wished she had him back so she could lean on his strength. Feel his arms around her, in comfort, just one more time.

It was a strange disconnect, though. If she still

had Sunil, she wouldn't have Leena. And she needed Leena.

Truly, marrying Alik was marrying for love. For the love of her child.

Then another thought occurred to her. One that made her feel scared and hot at the same time. She didn't know if it was angry heat, embarrassed heat, or something else entirely. It was the something else entirely that really worried her.

"You said there would be very little difference between my position as nanny and my position as wife. Were you planning on sexually harassing me as your staff or are you planning on keeping your hands off me if I'm your wife?"

"It is of no matter to me. If you want sex, I'm more than willing to give it."

The thought made a rash of heat spread over her skin. The way he said things like that, so bald and open, was something she just didn't understand. She wasn't a prude, but she wasn't going to start offering sex to a stranger either, as if it wasn't a bigger deal than choosing between pizza or dal for dinner.

"If *I* want sex?"

"You make it sound strange. Don't you like sex?"

She nearly choked. "I…I don't… It's not a recreational activity."

"Perhaps not to you." The smile that curved his lips told her he, indeed, thought of it as such, and she felt her toes curl in her shoes. Oh, good grief, he wasn't that hot. He was inappropriate. "Either way, the choice is yours. If you want it, I am willing."

"And if I don't?" she asked.

"As I said, it is of no matter to me. I'm not intending to pledge my faithfulness either way."

"You're not?" she asked, annoyed by that for some reason. Perhaps because in this plan, Alik seemed to be giving up nothing, while for her, everything was changing.

"I have a short attention span where women are concerned. My life is not conducive to relationships."

"I don't know that anyone's is. That's why people work at their marriages, you know?" For all that she'd loved her husband, they'd had their problems, but everyone in a long-term relationship did.

"Do you want my faithfulness?"

She half snorted half laughed. "Hardly."

"Then why make an issue of it? I won't demand yours, either. So long as Leena is cared for, I can't be bothered by what you do or who you're doing it with."

"Did you honestly just question whether or not I will care for Leena? I've been doing it for the past year—it's hardly going to change now. It's all I want to do. She's what I want."

"And because of that you have no interest in relationships?"

"I had a relationship," she said, feeling, for some reason, like claiming Sunil as a husband, considering the conversation, might cheapen it in some way. "He was all I ever wanted in a man, and he's gone now. That part of my life is gone. Over. Leena is my life now."

"Very noble of you."

"Hardly. I just know that I already had what a lot of people spend a lifetime looking for. No one gets that lucky twice."

He skipped over her words, as though he hadn't even been listening. "As I said, I don't care either way."

She felt numb. Light-headed. There was only one answer she could give.

"I will have to collect my things," she said, her words detached, as though they were being spoken by a stranger.

"I can send someone to do that for you."

Of course he could. He was a billionaire and all. "When would the marriage take place?"

"As soon as possible. In fact, I know just the place to have the wedding."

"Wedding?" she repeated, knowing she sounded dull.

"Of course we will have a wedding. We want it all to look authentic. For Leena's sake if for no other reason."

Just like that, she was treated with a welcome burst of anger. She stood from her chair, Leena still in her arms. "And your being seen with other women won't seem abnormal to Leena? I hope to God it does."

"She won't know about it," he said.

"How?"

He smiled, bright white teeth against tanned skin. "I'm a ghost, Jada. You don't read about me in the news, and there's a very good reason for that."

"You don't read about me in the news, either, and the reason is that I'm boring."

"Oh, I am not boring, and if the press ever got wind of me? I would be a headline." Coming from another man it would have sounded like bragging.

Like he was talking himself up. But Alik said it like he was stating the most mundane of facts. And it made her believe him. "As it is," he continued, "they know nothing about me, and I intend to keep it that way."

A shiver ran up her back, the hair on her neck standing on end. "You have a high opinion of yourself and your media appeal."

Granted, he would have media appeal in spades. Even if it was just because he had model good looks. She looked at him harder. No, perhaps he didn't have a model's good looks. Models usually possessed some sort of androgynous beauty, while Alik was hard. A scar ran through the center of his chin, one marring the smooth line of his upper lip. His hands were no better. Rough, looking as though the skin on the backs of them had been, at some point in his life, reduced to hamburger, and had since healed badly.

She hadn't noticed at first. She'd been too bowled over by his presence in general to take in the finer details. And now she was wondering exactly who this man was. This man she'd agreed to marry.

She had a feeling that she didn't really want to know.

"I'm simply realistic," he said. "However, ano-nymity suits me. It always has."

"Well, that's good, because it suits me, too."

"Glad to hear it." He picked up his cell phone and punched in a number. "Bring the car to the front of the coffee shop. And map the route to the airport."

"The airport?" Panic clawed at her, warring with despair for the position of dominant emotion.

"There is no need to wait, as I said."

"So, where are we going then? Paris? Barcelona or that town house in New York?" She tried to feign a bravado she didn't feel. Tried to find the strength she needed to survive this new pile of muck life had heaped onto her.

"Tell me, Jada, have you ever been to Attar?"

Attar was Alik's adopted country. The only coun-try he'd ever sworn a willing allegiance to. As a boy, pulled off the streets of Russia, he'd been asked very early on to betray his homeland, his people.

And he had done it. The promise of food and shelter too enticing to refuse. His conscience had burned at first, but then it burned past the point of healing. Singed beyond feeling.

Over the years he'd belonged to many nations. Taken the helm of many armies.

Attar was the one place he loved. The one place he called home. Sheikh Sayid al Kadar and his wife Chloe were a big part of that.

As his private jet touched down on the tarmac, waves of heat rising up to envelop the aircraft, Leena woke with a start, her plaintive wails working on his nerves.

He'd never been especially fond of children. Yes, he tolerated Sayid and Chloe's children, had sworn to protect them, but he hardly hung out to play favorite Uncle Alik, regardless of the fact that Sayid was the closest thing to a brother he'd ever had.

But then, he didn't anticipate spending too much time with his own child. The thought made him feel slightly uncomfortable for the first time, a strange pang hitting him in the chest. He wasn't sure why.

Because you know what abandonment feels like.

He shook off the thought. He wasn't abandoning Leena. He was shaking up his entire damned life to make sure she was cared for. And he was doing her a kindness by staying away.

"Welcome to Attar," he said. "We're on the sheikh's private runway, so there's no need to wait."

"The sheikh?"

"A friend of mine." His only friend.

"Well, I guess you are sort of newsworthy," she said.

She had no idea. His relationship with Sayid was only the tip of the iceberg, but he hardly intended to tell her about his past. He had no need to. They would marry, he would install her in the residence of her choice and then he would carry on as he had always done.

He made a mental note to put Leena's birthday in his calendar. He would attempt to make visits around that time. Failing that he would send a gift. That seemed a good thing to do. And it was a bloody sight better than abandonment.

He put his sunglasses on, prepared to contend with the heat of Attar, a heat he had grown accustomed to over the past six years. He suddenly realized that Jada and Leena weren't.

He pulled out his cell phone. "Bring the car up to the jet, make sure it is adequately cooled." It was strange, having to consider the comfort of others. He rarely considered his own comfort. He would have charged out into the heat and walked to where the car was, or walked on to Sayid's palace himself.

He grimaced. He didn't especially want to go straight to Sayid's palace. He would have the driver take him to his own palace.

"Wait until the car pulls up," he said to Jada.

"Why?" she asked.

"This is not the sort of heat you're used to."

"How do you know?"

"Unless you've spent years in a North African desert, it's not the kind of heat you're used to. I assume you have not?"

"Not recently," she said, her tone stiff. It almost struck him as funny, but he had the feeling if he laughed vulnerable body parts might be in danger.

"I thought you probably had not."

When he saw the sleek, black car pulling near the door of the plane, he gave the pilot the signal to open the door. The moment it started to lower, a wave of heat washed inside the cabin.

"You weren't joking," she said.

"No, I wasn't." The stairs were steep, and he wondered if a woman as petite as Jada could manage a wiggling one-year-old on her way down.

"Give her to me," he said.

"Why?"

"Do you want to try and negotiate those with her in your arms? If so, by all means." His discomfort with the situation, with the prospect of holding the child again, made his voice harder than he intended.

"And what makes you think you'll do better? You aren't experienced with babies. What if you drop her?"

"I have carried full-grown men down mountainsides when they were unable to walk for themselves. I think I can carry a baby down a flight of stairs. Give her to me."

Jada complied, but her expression remained mutinous.

"After you," he said.

She started down the steps and into the car, and he followed after her. There was a car seat ready in this vehicle, his orders followed down to the letter. There should also be supplies for a baby back at his home. Money didn't buy happiness—he knew that to be true. He doubted he'd felt a moment of true happiness in his life. But money bought a lot of conveniences, and a lot of things that felt close enough to that elusive emotion.

He much preferred having it to not having it. And a good thing, too, as he'd sold his soul to get it.

"Where are we headed?" she asked when the car started moving.

"To my palace." He looked out the window at the wide, flat expanse of desert, and the walls of the city beyond it. This was the first place he had ever felt at home. The desert showed a man where he was at, challenged him on a fundamental level. The desert didn't care for good or evil. Only strength. Survival.

It had been a rescue mission in this very desert that had nearly claimed his life. And now it was in his blood.

"You have a palace?"

"A gift from the sheikh."

"Extravagant gift."

"Not so much, all things considered."

"What things?" she asked.

He didn't know what made him do it, but he unbuttoned the top three buttons on his shirt and pulled the collar to the side, revealing the dark lines of his most recent tattoo. The one that covered his most recent scar.

Her eyes widened. She lifted her hand as though she was tempted to touch, to see if the skin beneath the ink was as rough and damaged as it looked. It was. He wanted her to do it. Wanted her to press her fingertips to his flesh, so he could see just how soft and delicate she truly was against his hardened, damaged skin.

She lowered her hand and the spell was broken. "Is that part of that newsworthiness you were talking about?" she asked.

"Some might say."

"It looks like it was painful."

"Not especially. I think the one on my wrist hurt worse."

"Not the tattoo," she said.

He chuckled, feeling a genuine sense of amusement. "I know."

They settled into silence for the rest of the drive. Jada stared out the window, her fingers fluffing his daughter's pale hair. He wondered if she looked like her mother. Her birth mother. He could scarcely remember the woman.

Based on geography he had a fair idea of who she was, but he ultimately couldn't be certain. A one-night stand that had occurred nearly two years earlier hardly stuck out in his mind. He'd had a lot of nights like that. A lot of encounters with women he barely exchanged names with before getting down to the business of what they both wanted.

He wondered if a normal man might feel shame over that. Over the fact that he could scarcely recall the woman who'd given birth to his child. Yes, a normal man would probably be ashamed. But Alik had spent too many years discovering that doing the right thing often meant going hungry, while doing the wrong thing could net you a hotel room and enough food for a week. He'd learned long ago that he would have to define right and wrong in his own way. The best way he'd been able to navigate life had been to chase all of the good feelings he could find.

Food and shelter made him comfortable, so whatever he'd had to do to get it, he had. Later on he'd discovered that sex made him feel good. So he had a lot of it. He was never cruel to his partners, never promised more than he was willing to deliver. And until recently, he'd imagined he'd left his lovers with nothing more than a smile on their face and a post-orgasmic buzz.

That turned out not to be strictly true. It made him feel unsettled. Made him question things it was far too late to question.

His palace was on the coast of Attar, facing the sea. The sun washed the sea a pale green, the rocks and sand red. And his home stood on the hill, a stunning contrast to the landscape. White walls and a golden, domed roof that shone bright in the midday heat.

Here, by the sea, the air was more breathable. Not as likely to burn you from the inside out.

"This is my home," he said. "Your home now, if you wish."

He wanted to take the invitation back as soon as he'd issued it. There was a reason he'd not mentioned the Attari palace in his initial list of homes Leena might live in. The heat was one reason, but there was another. This was his sanctuary. The one place he didn't bring women. The one place he brought no one.

Not now. Now he was bringing his daughter and the woman who was to become his wife. For the first time in his memory, he seriously questioned the decisions that he'd made.

CHAPTER FOUR

JADA COULD SCARCELY take in all of her surroundings. She clutched a sweaty, sleeping Leena to her chest and tried to ignore the heat of her daughter's body against hers, far too much in the arid Attari weather, and continued through the palace courtyard and into the opulent, cool, foyer.

"This is…like nothing I've ever seen."

"I felt the same way when I first came here. To Attar. It is like another world. Although, it's funny, I find some of the architecture so similar to what you find in Russia, but with dunes in the background instead of snow."

"Do you keep a home there?" she asked. She realized suddenly that it was not in the list of places he'd named earlier.

"I do," he said. "But I don't go there."

"Why?" The question applied to both parts of the statement. Why would he keep a home he never went to? And why would he not go there?

"I have no need to revisit my past."

"And yet you keep a house there?"

"Holding on to a piece of it, I suppose. But then, we all do that, do we not?"

"I suppose," she said. She flexed her fingers, became suddenly very conscious of the ring that was now on her right finger. She'd removed her wedding ring about a year after Sunil's death. And then a few months later she'd put it back on, but on her other hand. A way to remember, while acknowledging that the marriage bond was gone.

A way to hold on to a past that she could never reclaim. She knew all about holding on to what you couldn't go back to.

"I asked that my staff have rooms prepared for you and Leena. Rooms that are next to each other. I will call my housekeeper and see that she leads you to them."

"Not you?"

"I don't know where she installed you," he said, his total lack of interest almost fascinating to her. She wondered what it would be like to live like him. No ties, no cares. Even when it came to Leena, he seemed to simply think and act. None of it came from his heart and because of that there was no hesitation. No pain.

But there was also no conviction. Not true conviction. Not like she felt when she'd made the decision to come here, knowing that, no matter the cost she couldn't turn her back on her child.

As attractive as his brand of numbness seemed in some ways, she knew she would never really want it. There was no strength in it. Not true strength. It was better to hurt for lost love, and far better to have had it in the first place. Even in the lowest point of her grief she wouldn't have traded away her years with her husband. Even facing the potential loss of Leena, she would never regret the bond.

"Well, then how am I supposed to find you in this massive palace if you don't know where I am and I don't know where you are?" Everything about Attar was massive. The desert stretched on forever, ending at a sea that continued until it met sky. The palace was no less impressive. Expansive rooms and ceilings that curved high overhead. It made her long for the small coziness of her home. For the buildings back in Portland that hemmed them in a bit, the mountains that surrounded those.

Here, everything just seemed laid bare and exposed. She didn't like the feeling.

"I hardly thought you would want to find me," he said.

She had thought so, as well, but the idea of not

being able to find the only person she knew in this vast, cold stone building didn't sit well with her at all.

"Better than getting lost forever in this fortress you call a home."

He looked up, his focus on the domed ceiling. Sunbursts of gold, inlaid with jasper, jade and onyx. "A fortress? I would hardly call it that. I have spent time in fortresses. Prisons. Dungeons."

"I don't need to know what you do in your off time," she snapped, not sure what had prompted her to make the remark.

A slow smile curved his lips. "But what I do in my off time is so very fascinating. I'm sure you could benefit from a little off time yourself."

Her body reacted to the words with heat, with increased heart rate and sweaty palms. Her body was a filthy traitor. Her mind, on the other hand, came to her rescue. Sensible and suitably outraged.

"I already told you, I'm not going there with you. I've agreed to marry you, but I'm not sharing your bed. This marriage won't be real." It couldn't be real. She'd had a real marriage. A marriage filled with laughing and shouting and making love, and this, this union with a stranger, no matter that it was legal, would never be that.

There had been security in her marriage. Even at the low points, there had been an element of safety. Alik possessed nothing even slightly resembling safety. He was a law unto himself, much like the desert she found herself stranded in.

He crossed his muscular arms across his broad chest, one eyebrow arched. "On the contrary, this marriage will be very real in every way that counts."

Her skin prickled. "What does that mean?"

"All marriage is, is a legal document. But then, that's what adoption is, *da?* So you have to collect the proper legal documents to get your life in order. That's how I see it."

"That's not what marriage is."

"And you're an expert."

"Yeah," she said. "I am."

He stopped talking, his gray eyes locked with hers. "I do not claim expertise in that area. But all I'm saying is, it will be as real as it must be in order for you to make a permanent claim on Leena. That is all you require."

"Yes. Although I'm still a little unsure about why you're helping me."

Alik was, too. In some ways. In others…it made sense. It was what a family looked like. A mother and father, married. That was the traditional way of it. It was everything he'd never had, and he'd suffered for the lack of it. He would not allow Leena to suffer similarly.

And it was what Sayid had done. He had married Chloe in order to secure the future of his nephew and it had all turned out very well for him.

Of course, Alik wasn't counting on love and more children. He was in no danger of it, in fact. Love was something he had never managed to feel. Loyalty, yes. A bond of brotherhood with Sayid. But otherwise…no, love was certainly not on the table for him. It had been torn from him, the day his mother had left him in an overcrowded orphanage.

There could be no love but…perhaps a sort of facade of legitimacy. He hadn't been a soldier for hire in a long time. And since then, he'd parlayed his experience as a military strategist into the business world, and he'd been a huge success. But there were events, functions where people brought spouses or at least dates.

He'd never had an actual date. He didn't take women out, he met them out. At parties, clubs, and then he took them to bed. To whatever hotel room was closest. To the backseat of his car. He'd never been particular.

But things were changing. His life was changing. He'd long since abandoned some of the more self-destructive exploits of his youth. The truth was, being a soldier for hire had afforded him a lot of money. And in combination with being a man who didn't care whether he lived or died, it was a very dangerous thing.

Now though, things were different. He was ready for them to be, in some ways. He wondered if this was the thing that might finally reach the frozen block in his chest where his heart should be.

He'd spent years serving the lusts of his flesh, allowing his body to feel the things his heart simply could not.

He looked at the child in Jada's arms and he wished for a connection. For something. A recognition of her as his blood, as his family.

And there was nothing. No magic bond.

He gritted his teeth. "Yes, I think having you as a wife actually suits my purposes well. I've had a career change in the past few years and it will sometimes be good for me to have a wife to attend galas and things of that nature with me."

"Galas?"

"Yes."

"I didn't sign on to attend galas. I signed on to be a mother to my own child." He noticed that she adamantly continued to refuse to call Leena *his* child, "and to be left alone in one of your penthouses. In a location of my choosing, if I remember correctly."

"Perhaps I have changed what I expect. I ought to get something additional out of the deal, don't you think? And since sex isn't on offer I think the least you can do is put on a ball gown and hang on my arm at business functions."

She lifted her chin, lioness eyes glittering with deadly intent. "Whatever you wish, of course."

Such a dangerous acquiescence. He could tell she meant none of it, but that she was willing to play along with anything at this point. Anything to keep Leena close to her.

That realization made his chest burn, as though her conviction was so strong it had lit a spark within him. His child deserved that. This intense protectiveness, born of love, that Jada wore so proudly. And Leena would not get it from him. He could not give it.

All the better that Jada would be in residence.

"Somehow, I don't believe that," he said. "But I don't require your obedience."

"Don't you?"

He shrugged. "No. Where's the fun in that? I prefer women who like a challenge."

"I prefer you not think of me as a woman."

He looked over her petite figure. Small, perfectly formed breasts, gently rounded hips. "It's a bit late for that. It's the curves. They give you away."

She lifted her chin, golden eyes burning with fire. "I'm ready to see my room now."

"Then I shall call Adira."

Jada had been forbidden from putting her own things away by Alik's very stern head of the household. There were people for that sort of thing, and she was not to trouble herself. That extended to Leena's things. Both of which had arrived, inexplicably, only hours after they did.

Alik had made good on his every promise so far, which made it truly difficult to hate him too much.

Leena was his daughter, after all, and regardless of how she felt about his behavior, about how irresponsible one had to be to get into such a situation, she couldn't deny that he was Leena's father.

How could she deny Leena a chance to know

him? That Jada had been the one to love her and care for her did make her more important in her estimation, but the biological connection between Alik and Leena wasn't nothing.

The morality of the entire situation was sticky and horrible.

Jada sank onto her bed and watched Leena, toddling around the exterior of her blanket before sitting down a little bit too hard, her movements wobbly and clumsy. She didn't cry. She just clapped her chubby hands.

Jada slid off the edge of the bed and clasped one of Leena's hands in hers, ran a finger along the little dimples that disguised her knuckles. The price for this, for being with her daughter, wasn't too high.

There would never be a price too high. If she hadn't agreed to the marriage, to coming here with him, then she would have lost her child forever.

And if she'd agreed to be the nanny, she would have lost the position that was rightfully hers. After the doctors, she'd been the first person to hold Leena. She'd been the one who'd spent countless sleepless nights pacing the halls with a squalling child in her arms.

She was Leena's mother in every way that mattered. Marrying a stranger, leaving her home, her country, it was a small sacrifice for moments like these, and every moment in the future.

Leena was her life. Nothing else mattered.

"Settling in, I see."

Jada turned and saw Alik standing in the doorway. She hadn't heard him approach, hadn't heard the door to the bedroom open. He was almost supernaturally stealthy. It was a bit unnerving. But then, the man was unnerving in general.

"Yes. We are. I don't think Leena is fazed at all by the different surroundings."

"I think it would be different if you weren't here."

She blinked, not expecting the compliment. Not expecting him to understand. "You're very right about that."

"I made some calls. I was able to secure us a marriage license and it's all in order for the ceremony to take place this weekend."

Her throat tightened, her mouth going dry. "I imagine your connection with the sheikh helped on this one."

"It didn't hurt."

Why was the room spinning now? It seemed like it was spinning. "This morning, I woke up and got ready to go to the courthouse to finally get this adoption finalized. I thought, there's no way he'll get here in time and they'll just rule him as absentee. Now, I'm in a foreign country with a man I barely know, and I'm marrying him in three days." She said it all out loud, like it might help make it real. And if it wasn't real, maybe speaking out loud would wake her up from this bizarre dream.

"And this morning," he said, his voice quiet, "I got word that the hearing date had been changed and I went to a courthouse in another country, to make sure that I didn't lose the chance of ever seeing my own child. Knowing if I missed it, I may never even get a chance to look at her."

For the first time, she realized that Alik's life had been upended, too. Even if the upending was a result of his own actions. "I suppose we've both had a strange day."

He straightened. "To say the least." The gravity was now absent from his tone. "One of the strangest I've had, and if you were aware of my past history you would know that's saying something."

"I get that vibe from you."

"Do you?"

"Nothing about you seems typical."

Not even close. He was like a predatory animal in human form. Easy grace and harnessed power.

But with the ability to spring into action and tear out someone's throat in the blink of an eye. He'd looked at home in his denim and rumpled shirt, tattoos on display, and just as comfortable in a custom-tailored suit. He was a man who shifted identities as easily as breathing.

"I suppose not," he said. His words were oddly flat.

"So what is it you do?" she asked.

He looked surprised. For the first time since all of this had happened, since she'd met him, he actually looked caught off guard. "What do I do?"

"For work. For money. Other than…having sheikhs be indebted to you and gifting you palaces, that is."

"Right now? I'm a tactical expert. I go into corporations and help with strategies. How to take out the competition. Plans to increase productivity and profit. Whatever they need."

"Taking out the competition?"

A half smile curved his lips. Wicked. *Wicked* was the only word for that smile of his. "It's a clever little take on what I used to do, but that's another story."

"And do you do this for everyone? At some point aren't you working both sides?"

"Sometimes. But I am always one hundred percent loyal to whoever is paying for my services at a given time. It suits me. I don't want to man a massive corporation—I prefer to be a free agent. This allows me to move as I please."

"Given the financial information mentioned at the hearing you do very well at this."

"I do all right," he said.

Yeah. Eight figures of all right, but she wasn't going to say that. It was crass to talk about money, at least that's what her parents had always said.

"I'm just…I'm very tired," she said.

He looked down at Leena. "Will she sleep for you or shall I send one of my staff to help you?"

She felt drained suddenly. Incapable of doing anything but crawling into bed, pulling the covers over her head and trying to forget the entire day had happened. Trying to forget that this was her life.

She recognized this. Shock. Grief in a way. It was the loss of the life she'd planned for her and Leena.

"She'll be fine," she said. No way was she letting her daughter out of her sight. In fact, she doubted she'd even be using the adjoining room for her. She had a feeling she'd just pull the crib in and place it by her bed.

"As long as you're certain."

"I need her with me."

"Of course," he said. It was strange how he said it. His words lacked emotion. They lacked understanding. As though he didn't really get why she might need Leena close.

"I guess we'll talk more tomorrow."

"Yes. We will need to discuss wedding plans."

"I don't care about them," she said. "Hire someone else to do it."

"I was planning on it, but still, someone will have to come take your measurements. For your dress."

"Of course." She imagined he would put her in a Western-style wedding gown, which she found she actually preferred.

She'd had her big Indian wedding with Sunil. Worn the red sari she'd dreamed of since she was a little girl. Her extended family had all been there, her mother. She'd still had her mother then. It had been everything she'd wanted.

She would not let this wedding, this farce, infect the memory of *her* wedding. She needed this to be something else. Something different. A wedding that had no personal significance to her at all. Something that didn't feel like part of her.

"I want a white dress," she said.

"Tell the stylist when she comes tomorrow."

"I will."

As long as she kept it separate, someone else's wedding and not hers, maybe she could survive it.

CHAPTER FIVE

THE NEXT DAYS PASSED too quickly. No matter how hard Jada wished time would stand still, it simply wouldn't. And before she knew it, the day of the wedding arrived.

Why were they even having a wedding? For Leena, she knew, and then of course for Alik's peers. Wedding photos would be necessary for both.

It would be small, she'd been assured. Only Sayid and his family. Sayid, she'd found out, was the sheikh of Attar. So, only the sheikh. No big deal.

Jada felt like she would throw up.

She clutched the bouquet of lilies to her chest and looked down at the flowing, white fabric of her gown. She'd asked that everything be white. A total contrast to her first wedding, which had been filled with color, food and music.

She would have this feel as different as possible. As much like something other than her wedding as she could manage.

It wasn't working right now. Wasn't working to tame the butterflies that were rioting around in her belly.

There were more staff seeing to the wedding than there were people in attendance. It was almost funny. Between the photographer, the kitchen staff, the decorators, the coordinator and the minister, it was rather amazing.

They didn't have music. Her cue to walk up the aisle was when she could see Alik standing at the head of it. She peered around the gauzy curtain that separated the stone veranda from the walled gardens.

She could see him there. In a suit. No tie, the collar unbuttoned at his throat.

She almost turned and ran. But then she saw Leena. Leena in her little white dress, her chubby legs hanging over one of the chairs that had been set up around the altar area.

Chloe, Sayid's wife, was keeping an eye on her, along with her two children.

And that right there was why this was happening. It was why she was getting ready to walk down the aisle toward a man she didn't know. It was why she was going to do it with her head held high.

Because for Leena, she could do nothing less.

"You can do this, Jada," she whispered.

Then she swept the curtain aside and started down the aisle.

Alik wasn't certain what he'd expected to feel. Nothing, actually, that was what he'd expected to feel. That was the status quo after all.

But when he saw Jada, headed toward him, a white gown fitted over curves, white flowers pressed tightly against her chest, her dark hair covered by a frothy veil, he felt something.

Heat streaked through his veins, hot as fire and just as dangerous.

Lust.

He was well familiar with lust. But Jada was not a woman he wanted to feel any lust for. Keeping their arrangement purely on paper was essential. To the peace of his household, to the way he conducted his life.

Lust was something he simply couldn't afford.

And yet it was there, an insistent ball of heat in his gut. And when Jada came forward and placed her small, soft hand in his, golden and perfect against his own battered skin, it only stoked the flames.

She looked up, her eyes wide, as though she felt it, too. And was no happier about it than he was.

He had intended for her to have no effect on his life. And that was how it would remain. He kept that in the forefront of his mind as he spoke his vows. Repeated it mentally. No matter the words they spoke today, here at the altar, it would not change what he had planned.

It would not change his life.

But what if it does? That thought pushed against the ice blockade around his heart. And he shoved it away.

There was no kiss during the ceremony. It was not traditional to kiss publicly in Attar, and he felt that they should adhere to that part of the custom. He was exceedingly glad they had done so now.

As if a kiss could affect you?

After all he'd done, it should not have the power to do so. But he wondered. Wondered what it would do to him to touch his lips to hers. They were full, soft. So perfect looking. And he wanted a taste badly enough to know he'd made the right choice to exclude it from the ceremony. He'd bet she tasted like passion. Like emotion so deep he'd never reach the bottom.

He was used to women as jaded as himself, or

at least halfway to that point. But Jada was not that woman. He had to wonder...if he touched her, would it burn with heat like her eyes? Would it have the power to burn away the scars over his own emotions and set them all free?

The thought both intrigued and repelled him. It was a foolish thought. There was nothing that strong. Not even the fire of Jada's passion.

The wedding ended very quickly, and for that, he was grateful. The moment the pronouncement was made, that they were husband and wife, Jada left his side and went to where Leena was sitting, pulling the child into her arms.

He wondered if he would ever be able to do that so easily. If he would ever do it the way she did, out of necessity. If only that sort of connection, that sort of understanding could be transferred through a kiss.

But then what would be left of you if you lost your armor? Do you even know if there's anything underneath?

No. He didn't. And he had no intention of finding out.

Sayid came up from where he'd been sitting and joined Alik where he was standing, both of them watching their respective wives and children. That moment confirmed he had done right. His heart would not give him confirmation. It simply wasn't capable of it. But in his mind he knew, it was right.

"What have you done, Alik?"

"I did as you said I should do. I went and claimed my child."

"And the woman?"

"She is the woman who was trying to adopt Leena. I could hardly rip the child from her arms." Though that had been the original plan. Strange to think of it now. Strange to think he'd imagined it would work. To take Leena from Jada, when it seemed like they were a part of each other.

"Was she?" Sayid asked. "I did not realize there was someone who had been caring for her."

"Yes. Would that have changed your advice?" Alik was worried it might. That even Sayid would think Jada was better suited to the task.

"Not necessarily. How is it she ended up agreeing to marry you?"

"I told her to. It keeps her with the child. It creates a proper family. I did the right thing."

"You uprooted them both from their country. You forced a woman who has only known you for four days to marry you."

"Is it so different to what you did with Chloe?"

Sayid shot him a deadly look. "It was different."

"Not in the least."

"I had feelings for her when we married."

"I know," Alik said, mildly amused by the memory. He'd incurred the wrath of his friend by implying he'd been less than gentlemanly with the other man's wife in their brief time alone at his seaside palace.

"And you don't have feelings for this woman?"

"Of course not, Sayid, I barely have feelings." He flashed his friend his most practiced grin, the one that had gotten him out of more trouble than most people had ever been in.

"So you think."

"So I know."

"You told me once, Alik," Sayid said slowly, "that you saw no point in making vows you couldn't keep."

Alik shifted, the memory rushing back to him, making him uncomfortable. Because that was just what he'd done today. He'd made vows he had no intention of keeping. He had every intention of continuing on as he'd always done.

"I also told you that I avoid making vows whenever possible. Today, it was not possible." He looked over at Jada. She was sitting, holding Leena in her lap. Her golden skin had a gray tinge to it and her lips were chalky pale. She was miserable. The realization sent a pang straight to his chest. Strange. "This is different. She knows what this is."

"And you think that's enough? You think what happened here today, the words you spoke, you think those won't matter?"

"It is not the same as a normal marriage. It is to protect my daughter. To protect Jada's rights, which she insisted on. This makes sense."

Sayid laughed. "One thing you'll discover soon, my friend, is that women and children rarely make sense."

"I know about women."

"Yes, you do. But you don't know about wives."

Jada was sitting in her room, watching Leena sleep. Sayid and Chloe had lingered for a while, but as nice as they were, Jada had been happy to see them go. She was tired of being on show. Tired of playing the part of, if not happy bride, then at least contented bride. It was too much and the strain was starting to break her.

This whole thing might break her. She was afraid it would.

There was a light knock on her door. "Come in."

The door opened, and Adira appeared. Alik's head of the household was spare with her smiles but today, she offered Jada one. "Mr. Alik has requested that you join him for a late dinner."

"I…" With Adira looking at her like that she hardly felt like she could refuse. "What about Leena?"

"I will stay on this floor. If she cries, you will be fetched immediately." Adira was being friendly, but she had the air of a woman who brooked no nonsense, and would not be disagreed with. She reminded Jada a bit of her own mother.

"Thank you," she said.

She stood from her position on the bed and wondered if she should change again. She'd stripped off her wedding dress the moment she was up in her room, and had traded it out in favor of a simple sundress. She'd longed for the comfort of her sweatpants but it was way too hot to indulge herself.

No. She wasn't going to change. It didn't matter what she wore to see Alik.

Her husband. A vision of Alik swam through her head and panic assaulted her. No. She closed her eyes and thought the words again. Her husband.

And she willed an image of Sunil to appear. Alik was not her husband. Not truly.

She swallowed hard and patted the sleeping Leena once on her rounded belly before offering the housekeeper another smile and walking out of the room.

As she drew closer to the dining area, her heart started beating harder, faster. And she started remembering the wedding. The moment when Alik had taken her hand. His fingers had been rough on her skin, and hot, so hot. The heat had seeped through her skin, shot through her body, pooling in her stomach.

It had been so very like…

No. She wasn't even going to think it. He didn't turn her on. Yes, he was a handsome man, in his way. Well, *handsome* seemed wrong. *Handsome* sounded banal and safe. Vanilla. And Alik Vasin was anything but that.

He was scarred, rough. Dangerous. And in that danger, there was a magnetism that defied logic. That was unlike anything she'd ever experienced. Ever.

She blinked. Just thinking that felt like a betrayal. Not just to her marriage, but to who she was. She wasn't the kind of woman who lost her head over a hot man. A hot man she didn't even like. She idly wiped her palm on her skirt, trying to rid herself of the feeling of his flesh against hers. Trying to get rid of the heat.

It didn't work.

She walked down a curved staircase and a long hall, the high-gloss black floors casting a ghostly reflection in front of her. The palace was like a maze, and the week she'd spent there, mainly huddled in hers and Leena's rooms, hadn't been enough to make it feel familiar.

The one good thing about the size of the palace was that it made avoiding Alik simple. And all things considered, avoidance had been high on her list of priorities.

Her problem was simply that it had been too long since a man had touched her. Too long since she felt any sort of attraction or arousal. She simply hadn't been interested. She still wasn't, but it was nothing more than a body/brain disconnect. Nothing to get worked up about. She was still in control.

She took a shaking breath and walked into the dining room. Alik was sitting there, at the head of the table. The only light in the room was coming from flickering candles, set on the table, casting sharp shadows onto Alik's face.

She'd just been thinking that he looked dangerous. She'd had no idea. Until now. His cheekbones
looked more hard cut thanks to the flickering
flames, his jaw more angular. Harder. And his
eyes, they just looked hollow.

That, right there, should have been enough to
erase the heat.

And yet, for some reason, her palm burned all
the more.

"Do you feel rested?" he asked.

"I'm not really sure." She twisted her wedding
band, the one on her right hand. Not the one she'd
been given today. A reminder. Of what was real,
and what wasn't.

Then she took a seat somewhere in the middle of
the long, opulent banquet table. Sitting at the other
end made her look like a coward. And she was a
coward so she wasn't going to go sit next to him.

"I thought I should make sure you ate. You
touched nothing at the lunch after the wedding."

"I was too nervous to eat."

"You seemed very calm."

"I've learned not to show too much emotion on
the outside."

"Except that day at the courthouse."

She remembered vividly how she'd sat down and

cried on the floor. She wasn't even embarrassed about it. The thought of losing her daughter deserved that level of emotion. "Restraint was the last thing on my mind."

"Was everything at the wedding to your taste?" he asked.

"No," she said. "It wasn't. And that was my plan."

"Your plan?" He looked over at her and frowned. "Come sit closer to me. I'm not shouting down the table at you for our entire meal."

She complied reluctantly, again, because she didn't want to look like a coward, scooting toward him until there were only two chairs between them.

"Better?"

"Yes. Now tell me about this plan."

In order to tell him, she would have to talk about Sunil, and she'd been avoiding that. Because it seemed wrong to talk about him to Alik, the man she'd just made her husband. It was too complicated. Too confused.

"I… This was my second wedding."

"Was it?" His response wouldn't have sounded out of place if her previous statement had been "it was nice and warm today."

"Yes. I didn't want this one to resemble *my* wedding. This wasn't my wedding. Not in that way."

He turned the wineglass in front of him in a slow circle. "And what happened to your first husband?"

Leave it to Alik to ask so bluntly. Social niceties were not something he gave deference to. Although, she found she almost liked it. At least he asked for what he wanted to know. At least he spoke, even when the words were unpleasant.

Now *that* thought, the comparison she was making to her husband, that was a betrayal. She shut it down as quickly as it started.

"Sunil had a lifelong heart defect. At least that's what his doctor told me later. It had gone undetected until, one day his heart…stopped. He was at work. They took him to the hospital, kept him on life support for a while. But he never came back. He just slipped away."

"How long has it been?" he asked.

"Three years."

"You loved him?"

"I love him," she said. "Very much. Not…not in the same way, obviously. But, he will always live in my heart."

A knot of emotion formed in her chest, and she welcomed it. It was safer than the heat that had been blooming there only moments before. Much safer than any of the new, raw emotions she'd experienced in the past few weeks.

"I have never lost anyone I cared for like that. I can imagine it must be difficult for you."

For you. As if it wouldn't be for him. "You've never lost anyone you cared for?" She thought of her parents, of her husband. "You're very fortunate."

"I've never really loved anyone," he said, his tone cold, frightening in its flatness. "One good thing about that is it keeps you from loss."

"What about your parents?" she asked.

"I never knew them. My mother left me at an orphanage when I was two, probably nearly three. My date of birth is a best guess made by the woman working at the facility at the time I was brought in. My name was given to me in much the same way. I don't share my surname with anyone I'm related to. From there, when it became overcrowded I was put out on the streets."

"I…I'm sorry."

"No need to be."

Two servers came in and placed a tray in front of both her and Alik before leaving the room as quietly as they'd entered.

"It must have been hard," she said.

"It was all I knew. And as I think you must know, it's impossible to waste time feeling sorry for yourself when there is life to be lived."

She did know that. It had been one of the things that had made her most angry when she'd been at the lowest point in her grief. That life had gone on. That she'd still had to go to the grocery store, still had to eat. Pay bills. There had been no time to drown in her grief the way she'd really wanted to.

Now she saw that for the blessing it was.

"That's very true."

"I have been thinking," he said, his subject change sudden. "You should take my name. As should Leena."

"What? Why?"

"You don't want a different last name than your daughter, do you?"

"No…I hadn't…I hadn't considered it."

"You gave her her first name, and I will not change it, but I want her to carry my name. She is my only family. And you should carry it, as well."

"I don't…" Patel was her husband's name. Except, Sunil wasn't her husband anymore. Alik was. "I'm not sure I can do that." After what he'd just told her, about the orphanage worker who had chosen his name, she understood why it would matter to him.

But she couldn't do it. Not now. Changing her name was like changing herself, and she couldn't allow it. Couldn't allow this, couldn't allow Alik that sort of power.

"It is the most logical thing to do."

"I know," she snapped. "But I've just been so damn logical for the past week, that my heart has taken a beating and I'm not sure I can do this, too. I made you my husband today. That place belonged—belongs—to the man I loved. And if I take your name, then I have to get rid of his."

"It is no matter to me," he said, his tone hard. "It's entirely up to you. I thought you might like our family to share a name."

"A family? Is that what we are?" She hated herself for saying it. After what he'd just said, she knew she was stabbing at him, but she honestly couldn't stop herself.

"The closest thing to one I've had." Again, his voice carried that sort of detached weightlessness. As if none of this meant anything to him. As if he was simply relaying facts. The man seemed to live entirely in his head.

No, that wasn't really true. Because there was

something else about him. Something darker, much more frightening. Something earthy and sensual that came from a place deep inside of him. He was a man very much connected with his body, too.

And she didn't like how much her own body seemed to be intrigued by that.

"I will think about it. It doesn't have to be done right away. I can do it anytime."

"Of course. In the meantime though, I will give Leena my name."

"Leena Vasin," Jada said quietly. And she looked at the man across from her again, at the stubborn set of his jaw, the shape of his brow. She saw it then, for the first time. How had she missed it?

Leena looked so very much like her father. The expression she made when she was grumpy especially, favored the stern look on his face now.

"It suits her," Jada said, surprising herself when she said it. Surprised by how much she meant it.

Leena was Alik's daughter. There was no denying it or ignoring it. And she was glad in that moment that he was in her life. She was sure the feeling would come and go, but right now, she was glad that Leena had a father. Her father.

"Do you know," she said slowly, "she looks like you?"

Alik's eyes were obscured by shadow and it was impossible to see what he was thinking. "Does she?" His voice was inscrutable as ever. There was no way to get a read on his emotions. No way to know what he thought about that revelation.

"Yes. When she's about to throw a tantrum she gets a little crease between her eyebrows, just like you. And her eyes have more green in them, but they also have that gray that yours have."

"I hadn't noticed," he said.

"Neither had I until just now."

Alik looked down at his wineglass again. "We should eat before it gets cold."

"Yes," she said. She wasn't conscious of what she was eating, and the moment the plates were clear she couldn't actually remember what they'd been served.

"Would you like me to show you back to your room?"

Jada hesitated. It was dark now, no helpful light filtering in through the windows to guide her way. But the idea of traversing dark corridors with Alik didn't exactly make her feel extra safe.

It made her stomach feel tight, made it hard to breathe. Still, she didn't want to stumble around the palace for longer than necessary.

"Yes. Please, if you wouldn't mind."

Alik rose from his seat and Jada was reminded just how large he was, how imposing. Every inch the master of the castle. She didn't know why she found it so fascinating. Didn't know why she found him so fascinating.

He moved past her with that effortless grace of his. The deadly silence of a predator. It didn't seem possible that a man who was so large, so tall and broad, could be so quiet when he moved.

She followed him out into the dark hall and a shiver ran over her body, creeping up her arms, her neck. "Got a flaming torch you can tear off the wall and use to light our way?"

Alik paused and turned, his expression cast into shadow. The shivery feeling got a bit more pronounced. He extended his hand and placed it flat on the wall, and then…the lights came on. And the expression revealed on his face could only be called *smart-assed.* "I could do that," he said, "but it would be so much easier to simply find the light switches."

"That would have been nice to know about earlier, so I wasn't walking through this medieval heap in the dark."

He turned away from her and started down the

hall again, his back, wide and muscular, filling her vision. "Why on earth would I live in a place that didn't possess modern conveniences? I've been homeless. I've been in prisons. I've done my time without modern luxury, and I find it isn't my favorite."

"You've been in jail? How is it that the court deemed you a more fit parent than I am?"

"I don't think it was a question of who was more fit, so much as who was more related. But, if it soothes you, the court didn't see any criminal record."

"How is that possible?"

"First of all, I doubt the Russian Mafia keep a record of every snot-nosed street kid they've locked up for a few days to teach a lesson to. Second, I'm skeptical that any of the guerrilla military factions I found myself on the unfriendly side of reported my prison time to the United States—or any government. Also, records and things like that may have been sanitized by some grateful rulers and the occasional victorious revolutionary."

She stopped in her tracks and he kept on walking. "Wait a second. What is it you used to do?"

"What I do now for corporations? I used to do

that for governments. Or, as I said, revolutionaries. Whoever offered the money."

"You were a mercenary." For the first time, she realized that the little prickle of hair on her arms, that vague sense of danger, wasn't ridiculous. Alik Vasin was, or had been, a very dangerous man. And she had just married him.

"I suppose that's the job title, though I was never too bothered about being specific with that. Didn't exactly fill out tax forms. But that's another thing I won't be advertising to the courts."

Jada curled her fingers into fists, her nails digging in her palms. "I don't imagine there's a box to check for that on official forms."

"Not so much."

"How did you…how did you get into something like that?" She was curious, even though she knew she shouldn't be. What she should be, was running away, and yet, for some reason, though that feeling of danger emanating from him remained, she wasn't afraid of him.

"I told you, I was an orphan. I crossed paths with the Russian Mafia quite by accident one day when I was picking pockets. After teaching me a sufficient lesson," he said, one long finger drifting over a scar that ran the length of his jaw, "the man I had attempted to rob asked how I'd done it so well. You see, he didn't feel me lift his wallet. He was told by his guards, who were walking behind him. Who I was walking in the middle of."

"What did you say?"

"I explained to him my process. The way I waited for the crowds on the street to be at a certain peak, how I waited for my mark to be at a certain point in their stride. And I told him, that when I was about to go for the grab, everything slowed down, and it was just effortless. He liked that."

"And he had you picking pockets?"

"Hardly. But I was twelve and what he saw was the mind of a strategist. He was right. I had a gift for seeing all angles of a scenario, except, of course, in the instance where they caught me. I missed seeing that he had guards with him. That's always bothered me."

"It has?"

"No one likes to lose. Anyway, that was the start of my career in organized crime. They helped me hone my abilities and then they exploited them. Until I became too recognizable in Moscow. Until I got tired of playing the game. This was when I was maybe sixteen or so. But I left them with a lot of money in my pocket, though I have to say I'm not overly keen on wandering the streets in my hometown alone. I don't trust how far that goodwill we parted with extends."

"Then what?" In spite of herself, she was fascinated. She should be scared, but she wasn't. Not really.

He started walking again and she jogged into place behind him to keep up. "Then, I found out I had a reputation. A man found me when I was in Japan and asked me to do a job. To help a militia overthrow a very oppressive government."

"And you helped them."

"The price was right. I'm not a charity."

"But you did the job."

He nodded once. "I did. And I did it successfully. After that, word spread."

"And that's what you did after that? Hired yourself out as a…weapon?"

"For some years."

"And then?"

"I had a mission here in Attar. To try and secure the borders. And for the first time, the mission went wrong. Sheikh Sayid was taken captive." It was the first time she'd heard even a glimmer of true emotion in his voice. "And though I was offered another check, another job, I knew I couldn't leave him there."

"You cared for him."

"I was the head of the mission—if it went wrong it was on me. When I take money to aid a certain faction then I am loyal to that faction until the job is done. The job wasn't done."

"And you cared for him."

"Sayid is the most honorable man I have ever met, in a life spent surrounded by men who would sell their grandmothers for a chance at their version of glory. It was refreshing to meet someone who had nothing but loyalty to his family, to his country, no matter what he could achieve elsewhere. Sayid was taken into captivity because he deviated from the mission. Because he stopped a woman from being assaulted by two soldiers. I would not have done the same in his position, because at that time in my life, all I saw was the mission. The plan. And Sayid made me look past that for the first time."

Jada felt something shift around her heart. Dear heaven, she wasn't starting to understand this man, was she? She'd grown up in a comfortable, middle-class home in the U.S. Born to parents to who had risked everything, left their homeland, to build a better life for their children. How could she understand a man who had spent his life alone? A man who had witnessed, and very likely committed, terrible acts of violence? It made no sense.

And yet, for some reason, she felt she did understand. She wasn't sure why, or how…if it came back to hormones and the fact that he was just muscular enough to lull her into a stupor.

Except, her hormones weren't centered around her heart, and that was definitely where a good portion of the feelings were coming from. She felt for him. Sad, happy that he'd found Sayid. And the real danger lay in the fact that she wanted to know more. That she was curious about him. About what was beneath the layers of rock that he kept between himself and the world.

Because there were layers. All shields were up with this man, no question. As he'd relayed the story of his desolate childhood, his life as a mercenary, there had been no emotion. Until the mention of Sayid.

"And that's how you ended up with a palace in the desert?"

"That is the long version of the story, yes. The short version is, a sheikh gave me a palace. Women like that one, usually," he said, giving her a careless wink before turning away, taking a right at the curved staircase that would lead them back to her room.

"I'm sure they do. What do they think of the whole ex-mercenary thing?"

"Oh, I don't go spreading that one around."

"What do you tell them you do?"

"They don't usually ask."

"They don't?"

"No," he said.

She had to take two stairs at a time to try and keep up with his long stride. At only five three, she wasn't exactly long legged, and she guessed he was more than a foot taller than she was. "What do they ask?"

He stopped and turned to her and she didn't manage to stop her stride in time, putting herself right in front of him, her eyes level with the center of his chest. "They don't usually talk this much," he said, eyes intent on hers.

She sucked in a shuddering breath, suddenly finding it hard to stand straight. She'd never been so close to a man who was so…so much. That's what it was. Alik was just too much. Too masculine, too unrefined, too sexy. Oh, he was much too sexy. He was also too immoral, too unemotional and too much a stranger for her to be going weak-kneed over him.

Yet again, her body didn't seem to care much for the common sense take on things.

"I see."

"Do you?" he asked, his head cocked to the side.

"Y-yes."

Why wasn't he moving? She couldn't back up, then she would betray that she was unnerved by his closeness. She was, but he didn't need to know that. He needed to move on up the stairs so that she could breathe again. So that her body would feel like it belonged to her again.

"You don't approve," he said, turning away and continuing up the stairs.

The knot that had been building in her chest frayed and loosened, releasing a gust of air from her lungs. "I'm not judging," she said.

"You are judging."

"Only a little. Because clearly, Leena as evidence, you have some control issues when it comes to women."

"I do not have control issues," he said.

"Really?" They reached the top of the stairs and Alik didn't turn on any lights.

"Really," he said, crossing his arms over his

chest. "Saying I have control issues implies that I fail at stopping myself from conducting liaisons with women when the simple truth is, I give in willingly. Unless I'm on duty, I don't see the point in abstaining."

"I don't even know what to say to that. And I don't believe that that's sufficient evidence that you don't have an issue with control. I find you self-indulgent."

"I am extremely self-indulgent. And also quite indulgent of my partners. But it still doesn't speak to a lack of control." He took a step toward her, and she took one away from him. Her back came up against the wall and her breathing stopped altogether.

"I think it does," she said, unwilling to back down.

"Oh, Jada, if I had a lack of control—" he advanced on her again, and she found herself without anywhere to flee "—you would know."

"I would?" She cursed her mouth. It was part of the mutiny against common sense her body was currently executing while her brain looked on in horror.

"I would have kissed you by now. I would have pulled you into my arms and tasted your lips, your throat. I would have put my hand on your breast, felt your nipples getting hard beneath my fingers. Then my tongue."

She turned her head to the side. It was the only way she could force herself not to look at him, the only way to keep herself from being drawn into his web.

He chuckled and she looked back. He had moved away from her, continuing on down the hall. "Lucky for you," he said, "I have no such control issues."

Insults flooded her mind, insults that wanted badly to escape and fly at his head. However, for some reason, now she had some sort of handle on her self-control and she couldn't speak them. A cruel joke.

It took her a moment, but she could finally speak again. "I wouldn't let you."

"I'm not so sure that's true," he said, stopping at a door that looked very much like the rest of the doors to her. "This is you."

"So it is," she said, still not convinced. Everything looked the same to her and this place was like a maze. "And I *wouldn't* let you."

He looked at her, and she felt every heated word he'd said pouring into her. Felt it beneath her skin, promises of sensual pleasure that went well beyond her experience.

She didn't know where that thought had come from. She knew about sex and she'd had plenty of it. She seriously doubted that there was sensual pleasure she somehow hadn't reached. Sex was all fine and good, but not, in her experience, something to make you lose your mind. And there was no way the experience would be better with Alik. She'd loved her husband, after all, and she didn't even like this man.

Love made sex better, surely. Love was what she'd waited for. Love and marriage, and there had been no one since. Because emotion was more important than desire and she understood that. She almost pitied Alik for not getting it.

And she pitied her poor, traitorous body its increased heart rate and sweaty palms. She was above all that. She knew better than to be drawn into it.

"If you say so," he said. "Have a good night."

"I will." *Alone.*

"I will see you tomorrow."

She didn't want to see him tomorrow. She wanted to pretend that in the morning, all of this would evaporate. But she'd been hoping that for days now, and still, every morning she woke up in a palace in a foreign desert country, the sea crashing outside of her window.

And while, on paper, that all sounded fine, the inclusion of Alik Vasin made it feel decidedly less so.

CHAPTER SIX

THERE WAS NO GOOD REASON for Alik to remain in
Attar, and remain celibate. None at all. And yet,
here he was, still tethered to his palace and, in effect, to the woman and child who were occupy-
ing it.

It had been a strange couple of weeks. It had, at
first, been easy to justify that he was staying to
ensure he didn't subject the child to another move
too quickly after the first one. Then he'd had to
wait for the adoption paperwork to come for Jada
so he could sign anything he needed to sign and
they could get everything sent in. Then, he thought
he shouldn't leave them here. It was too remote.
He would feel more comfortable, a bit like less of
a marauding bastard, if he installed them in one
of his more urban homes.

So that Jada could walk or drive where she
needed to go. So that they didn't have to worry
about sandstorms or any of the other dangers in
the desert. And there were so many.

Alik paced the length of the balcony that looked out over his pool. That pool was one of the dangers. As was a balcony. He would have to be sure everything was secured.

He hadn't known there were so many dangers in the world until he'd brought a child into his life. Laughable though the thought was, since he was a man who had faced death more times than most. But thinking of danger in the context of himself didn't bother him in the least.

But that soft, small, helpless little girl who now lived in his home? Thinking of her in danger twisted his insides.

And there were so many dangers to a person that small. The floors in the palace were too hard. The stone a hazard for a toddling child's forehead.

Alik strode back into his room and down the stairs. Jada was sitting in the dining room, holding Leena in her lap. Leena had her chubby fist wrapped around a piece of banana.

"Babies are impractical," he said.

Jada arched one dark eyebrow. "How so?"

"They are too small. It's unreasonable."

"Do you think so?" she asked, her eyes glittering with amusement. It irritated him.

"Yes."

"You should have seen her when she was a new-born. She weighed six pounds. She was no longer than your forearm."

He looked down at his arm. "That is entirely un-reasonable."

"But so cute."

"They are also loud. Too loud for something so small."

"The better to keep track of them."

"That is practical."

Jada smiled, and Alik felt a strong tug in his gut. More impractical even than babies, was his attraction to his new wife. She was beautiful, so it was no real surprise that it existed. It was the insistence of it. The total, consuming nature of it. He wasn't accustomed to giving a woman more than a passing assessment and, if she was willing, acting upon the attraction, or walking away if she wasn't.

Although, in his memory there had been no un-willing women. Women typically responded to him. It was almost predictable. The kind of pre-dictable he would never complain about. Perhaps that was the difference. Jada didn't want him, or rather, didn't want to want him, with a vehemence that emanated from her petite frame.

It was unusual. And not as deterring as he would have liked it to be.

He should stay well away from her. That he felt the desire to kiss her, to steal some of that passion from her, was warning enough that she was the sort of woman he should never touch. The level to which she tempted him should be warning enough.

"I'm glad you find something about your daughter to be practical," she said.

"It wasn't a commentary on her, but on all new humans. The head size is also of concern to me."

"Of concern to you? Think of how concerning it is for women—we have to give birth to them."

"You didn't."

He realized the moment he said the words, that they had been wrong. He had never spent much time being concerned with whether or not his words were hurtful or right. He'd never had to. He wasn't in the habit of making much in the way of conversation with anyone. Only Sayid had his ear.

Otherwise, in the rooms filled with the most people, there was rarely anything to say. In clubs everyone was too busy dancing, letting the music move through their bodies and erase everything else. Failing that, there was the alcohol chaser— he was a big fan of those.

But there wasn't conversation. And as he'd always seen himself as being smooth, adept, he was shocked to discover that conversing with women was not his strength. Which made it an even bigger shame that sex with Jada was off the table. Because, in the bedroom at least, he would satisfy her, of that he was certain.

"That was a jackass thing to say," she said, standing up, Leena held firmly against her chest.

Frustration bubbled up in him. He wished he could understand things like this. Emotion. He'd spent the better part of his life faking it, expecting that one day it would take root down inside of him, but it hadn't. It left him feeling at a disadvantage in these types of situations. And he hated feeling at a disadvantage.

"I know," he said. Because he did know, even if he didn't understand why.

"Then why did you say it?"

"I was merely making an observation."

"Don't make observations like that."

"Explain to me then, why it was the wrong thing to say."

She looked shocked, and angry. Her dark brows were locked together, eyes glimmering with golden fire. "You need it explained to you? Why your need to undermine me as Leena's mother is offensive? I didn't marry you to be treated like the help. I married you so that my position as Leena's mother would be unquestionable. To you and to everyone else. So your comments about how I didn't give birth to her only serve to take that sacrifice and make it meaningless!"

"How is it made meaningless by a comment? I didn't physically destroy the marriage license, or any of the adoption paperwork, and that is what gives you your status."

Logic. He would try and use logic to defuse the situation.

Judging by the stormy look on her face, it didn't work.

"That's your problem, Alik. You see things in black-and-white. You see them as blood or paperwork without taking the heart into the equation, and you can't do that." She turned and walked from the room, leaving him standing there alone.

Why the hell hadn't he left? He could get some peace and quiet. Stop worrying about Leena bumping her head on the stone floors.

He could find a woman. He could go and get laid and stop obsessing about Jada.

He took his cell phone out of his pocket and

dialed his personal assistant. "Luca, forward my calls. I will be here in Attar working for the foreseeable future."

He punched the end call button and sat down at the table. He put his palm on the table and into a spot of mushed banana. He grimaced. "Coffee!" he shouted, not caring he sounded demanding. He had to have control over something.

Because he seemed to have lost control over a hell of a lot since Jada Patel had entered his life.

Leena was sound asleep, and Jada found she envied her daughter. Leena didn't have any cares. She slept soundly and with a clean conscience, while Jada paced around in the dark feeling overheated and guilty. And a little dirty.

She should be upset at Alik. She *was* upset at Alik. But what she shouldn't be was attracted to Alik, and she found that no matter how stupid and offensive the things that came out of his mouth were, the feelings didn't go away.

They hadn't been instant. Not anywhere near it. She'd been too angry with him, had hated him too much initially. She wasn't sure she liked him a whole lot more now, but being in proximity with him had given her time to notice what she hadn't at first.

And that was basically a chiseled jaw, flawless muscle structure and eyes that seemed to see straight through her. Or at least straight through her clothes. Which, again, should be much more offensive than it was.

She huffed and walked out of her bedroom, closing the door gently behind her, and heading down the stairs, out to the garden area. The palace was still hard for her to navigate, less so now that she'd realized it had light switches. The memory made her smile and she forced herself to stop. No dreamy, smiley-type memories of Alik.

It was manufactured. Because if she went further with that memory, she would come to the crude, awful things he'd said to her in the hall. About kissing her. Touching her.

Her body heated. With rage, she was sure. Because it had been crude. Not exciting.

She pushed open the ornate double doors that led out to the pool and the gardens. She paused and headed toward the pool, which was set into the balcony, overlooking the ocean.

She stopped when she heard the sound of water in motion, closer than the waves below. And she had to wonder if she'd come here on purpose, hoping a little bit that she might find him.

He hadn't seen her yet, though. There was no way.

She could just barely make out his shape. He was gliding through the water, a dark shadow in the brightly lit pool. Like a shark. She had to stop comparing him to predators—it was giving her a complex. Making her feel hunted.

Another rash of heat spread through her. What was wrong with her? Where was sensible, practical Jada?

"Jada." His head was above the surface now and he was treading water, his eyes fixed on her.

"How do you do that?" she asked.

"If I was not good at sensing when people were present, I would be dead by now."

"You say that with such certainty."

"I am certain of it." He swam to the edge of the pool, planting his palms firmly on the side and levering himself out of the water.

She watched the play of his muscles, water sliding down over the dips and hollows. Her throat felt suddenly dry and she realized she was thirsty. That brought to mind the image of her sliding her tongue over his skin, collecting the drops and…

She blinked. "I couldn't sleep," she said. "Obviously neither could you."

"Not so much." He reached down and took a towel from one of the chairs that lined the pool, dragging it over his broad chest. Her eyes followed the motion.

She could see now, more clearly, the tattoo on his chest, and when he raised his arm to brush the towel over his short dark hair, she saw another one, words, running the length of his bicep.

"What do they mean?" she asked.

"This one?" he pointed to the inside of his wrist, the black anchor. "Nothing. I was very drunk that night."

"And the one on your chest? It's written in Arabic, isn't it?"

"Yes. I got it after that hideous injury healed. I don't often complain about pain, but that one hurt." He paused. "It was after Sayid was taken captive. He was in prison for a year. That's how long it took us to find him. A year of intel, of threats and whatever else we could do to convince his enemies to reveal his whereabouts. I got it just before we executed the mission to rescue him. It's a common proverb here, something parents say to their children. 'At the time of a test, a person rises or falls.'

I knew that when I went in after Sayid, I would rise or fall with him. Luckily, we lived."

"Yes, luckily."

White teeth flashed in the darkness, one of his naughty smiles, she was sure. "You don't sound overly thrilled about me coming out of it alive, Jada."

"I wouldn't wish death on you. Not on anyone. I'm glad Leena has a father." Though she wished Leena could have a father more capable of loving her. Alik cared, she could see that. There was a fierce protectiveness that ran through his actions with his daughter, but there was no tenderness. He almost seemed afraid of her. Afraid to touch her.

She thought back to their earlier conversation about babies and wondered if he was worried that she'd break beneath his touch.

"You just wish it wasn't me," he said. There was emotion beneath his words, and she was startled by it. She was used to cool detachment from him, from a logical approach to things that simply couldn't be reasoned out, in her opinion.

She shook her head. "Not necessarily."

"She would be your husband's daughter, if he were still alive."

She closed her eyes and fought a wave of sadness as it washed over her. Typical of Alik to say, with overwhelming casualness, the most hurtful thing. And to not even realize or understand it. No, Sunil wouldn't have been Leena's father. Because with him, she wasn't sure adoption would have ever happened. Thinking about that just confused her. Hurt her.

"But he's not." She opened her eyes again. "He's not here. He's not her father. And I've moved on from that."

"You have moved on?"

She blinked, knowing her next words would be a lie. "Yes."

"How? Explain to me how you have moved on? You have had other lovers?"

She hadn't even been on a date. Hadn't looked at another man. Hadn't wanted to. Until Alik. And since she'd met him she still didn't *want* to look at another man, she was just finding it difficult not to. "No. I was focused on the adoption."

"Then how is it you've moved on?"

"How do you move on?" she asked. She knew he wouldn't know. He didn't understand things like that. Things like emotion and pain, things like what it meant to love someone. "I mean, really. That part of my life is a part of me. It's who I am."

"And what do you mean by that?"

"I spent most of my adult life being his wife. Learning how to live with him, as you do with any marriage. Cooking food just how he liked it."

"Making love how he liked it?"

Her cheeks burned. "That too."

"And what about what you like?"

"Marriage is compromise," she said. "You give, your spouse gives. You form a new shape to accommodate them. And then when you lose them…"

"The changes don't make sense?"

She nodded slowly. "Something like that."

"She would, perhaps, be better off with your first husband than with me."

His tone was rough now, an edge to it.

"I don't resent your place in Leena's life," she said, realizing that it was true.

"I think you do."

"No, Alik. I only resent your place in my life."

"I see. And what about it do you find so objectionable?"

"You're my husband," she said, her voice cutting itself off, choking itself out. "And you shouldn't be."

"Tell me honestly, did you ever plan to marry again?"

"No."

"Then why does it matter what title I have. You are all about the heart, Jada, in which case, to you, no matter if I'm your husband on paper, the fact that I'm not your husband in your heart is all that should matter."

But it did. She wanted to scream it. Wanted to shout it to the heavens so he would understand. It mattered because only one man should ever have had the title. It mattered, but it shouldn't. She knew that.

Signing a document wasn't what forged a bond between people, and yet…there was something. Husband was still a meaningful position whether she wanted it to be or not. That was the real problem. Not that she felt nothing, but that she was starting to. And maybe it was down to Leena, to their connection with her.

That she could handle. Yes, they should feel bonded over Leena. They both wanted what was best for her and had acted in her best interest. So of course, they would feel a connection. Not that he did—she doubted Alik was bothered with her at all. But with her maternal instinct and all, it was logical she would feel something.

And that was all. She was sure of it.

"I don't know how you can be so calm about it. This is hardly how I saw my life going."

"Maybe then, that is the difference between you and me. I didn't see my life going anywhere."

"What does that mean?"

"Every day I got up and didn't count on making it back to my bed that night to sleep. I lived every day like it would be my last one, and sometimes I made an attempt to make it my last one. Oh, not actively, but safety has never been high on my list of priorities. So it's very hard to be disappointed at how your life has turned out when it's a surprise that you're still living at all."

His words chilled her down to her bones, and at the same time, the fire that was blazing in his eyes ignited her soul. She had always planned, always worried. Had always held life close to her chest like the precious gift that it was. And she had gotten so much pain, so many carefully laid plans utterly destroyed. What would it be like to be covered in a layer of armor as thick as Alik's? Would things roll off? Would life feel easier? She imagined that it might. Things had been so hard for so long she could hardly imagine what it might be like to have it just be simple for a while.

Alik's life certainly wasn't easy—it wasn't even

terribly happy and yet he seemed so much more at ease with all of it.

"Failing that," he said, his voice getting rougher, deeper, causing everything in her to respond to it, "I could always try and make you feel more married to me."

He took a step toward her and she knew what was going to happen. She also knew that she should tell him to stop. That she should be good and sensible. That she should ignore the rapid beat of her pulse, and the tightening in her stomach. That she should embrace logical thought, and reason.

But she didn't. She just stood and watched him advance, her throat dry, her breath coming in harsh, shallow bursts.

Why wasn't she running? Why wasn't she telling him no?

Because I don't want to.

He hooked his arm around her waist and pulled her up against his body. Water from his bare skin soaked through her cotton top, the chill making her nipples tighten. She wasn't wearing a bra because she'd been dressed for bed and now she was unbearably conscious of the fact and, heaven help her, grateful.

He cupped her chin with his thumb and forefinger, forced her to meet his gaze, and a flame burst to life inside of her. She wanted, so much it was painful, the need hot, raging, threatening to destroy everything if it wasn't met.

The tip of his thumb touched her lips, and she opened her mouth, tasted the salt on his skin from the water drops. She sucked on him, gently, and a rough growl came from deep in his chest. He tightened his hold on her and pulled her in tight, and in one fluid motion, he dipped his head and started kissing her.

Deep, sensuous, his tongue sliding against hers, tracing the line of her lips, before delving deep again. She'd never been kissed like this. So hard, so desperate. She didn't know where the hunger had come from. And then she had to wonder if it was coming from her.

This kiss was different because she had never wanted like this. Had never craved a man in quite this way.

She flattened her palms on his chest, his skin slick, hair roughened and hot beneath her hands. And she could feel his heart, throbbing fast and hard, proof that he felt it, too. That he felt the intensity like she did.

He lowered his hand and palmed her butt, drawing her in closer, bringing the V at the apex of her thighs into contact with the hard evidence of his desire. She moved her hands off his chest and looped them around his neck, forking her fingers through his hair, holding him tight.

His hand slid upward and then down the waistband of her sweatpants, beneath her underwear. She gasped when his callused palm cupped her skin, and she sighed when he squeezed her tight, amping up the tension, her need, making her ache for him.

He pushed his other hand beneath her top, found her breast, squeezed her nipple tight before sliding his thumb over it. She arched into his touch, raking her nails over his back and letting her head fall back. He took advantage of her exposed throat, pressing hot, openmouthed kisses to her skin.

He pushed his hand up higher and managed to strip her of her top in one easy motion, then he kissed her mouth again, deeper, harder, and she couldn't think. Couldn't remember why she'd ever wanted to run from this. Couldn't remember why she was here or even who she was. All she knew was that she wanted more. Whatever he would give, she wanted more.

He moved his hand down from her butt, pushing it between her thighs, sliding his fingers between her slick folds. If she could have thought, she would have been embarrassed over just how obvious it was that she wanted him, over just how ready she was, so fast. But she couldn't think past the burning pleasure that was arcing along her veins.

One finger slid over her clitoris and she pulled her mouth away from his, a strangled cry, too loud in the still of the night, escaping her lips, pushing against the haze of fantasy she'd built up to block out reality.

And then it hit her, with full, hideous force. She was half-naked, outside, with a man she barely knew and she was about to let him have sex with her.

She pulled away from him, gasping for air, looking around frantically for her shirt. She ran through a litany of curse words just under her breath while she bent to retrieve her top and tugged it over her head.

"What happened?" Alik asked.

"What happened? You kissed me and then thirty seconds later you were stripping me naked and… touching me."

"Are you going to pretend that you didn't like

it?" he asked. "Because I have a low tolerance for things like that."

"I don't do things like this."

He looked at her, slow, appraising. Making her hot all over again. "Maybe you should, because you're very good at it."

She frowned, wrapping her arms around herself, a shiver racking her frame. "What's that supposed to mean?"

"That I enjoyed kissing you. And touching you. And I would very much enjoy taking it to its logical conclusion."

"But to what end?" she asked.

He frowned. "Orgasm, what else?"

She let out a short, frustrated growl. "Is that all that matters to you? Not if we mess up what we're trying to build for Leena, but having an orgasm?"

"Why would it mess anything up?"

"Are you truly so obtuse?" She examined the look on his face, totally blank, totally unruffled, and she suddenly started to understand. "It would honestly make no difference to you, would it?"

"What we do in the bedroom would be separate from how we raise Leena."

"But sex isn't separate from a relationship—it's

woven through it. You can't simply ignore it during the day."

"Why not? I don't see how sex is connected to the day to day. It's a release, an adrenaline rush. My favorite way to get one, in fact, but it hardly affects what I do with the rest of my time."

"And that's why we can't. Because I can't separate it. Because I know what it can mean. How close it can make people. And you never will."

"I don't feel I especially need to know it."

"I know, Alik. And that's another problem." Jada crossed her arms beneath her breasts and walked back into the house, making a concerted effort not to look back at him. That might look like longing. It might look like she regretted the decision to stop. And she didn't. She couldn't.

This kind of thing might be fine for some people. It might be fine for Alik, but it wasn't her. Love was stronger than lust; it was more important. No matter how much she might think she wanted Alik, that was just physical. And the physical wasn't all that important.

She liked the physical, but you couldn't cuddle up with the physical afterward. And it wouldn't sit and have pancakes with you in the morning. Wouldn't hold you when you cried. The physical was only good for one thing, and she just didn't live her life that way.

It wasn't her.

Of course, that meant she would be living the rest of her life feeling very physically unsatisfied. Because she wasn't doing love again. And without love, she wasn't doing sex.

She bit her lip, fighting against a wave of unresolved arousal, and tried not to think about how very much she'd wanted to cast off her inhibitions and live life like Alik, if only for one night.

Alik prowled the length of his office, his entire body on red alert, an adrenaline high on a level he'd never experienced outside of the battlefield.

What was wrong with him? And what was wrong with her? Clearly she'd wanted him, so what was the point in denying it? It made no sense to him.

He pushed his hands back through his hair and noticed that his phone was blinking. He snatched it up off his desk. "Vasin."

"I expected to get voice mail."

"I was awake. What is it?"

"This is Michael LaMont. We spoke a few weeks ago."

"I remember," Alik said, gritting his teeth. As if he would forget.

"I was wondering if you'd given any more thought to taking up my cause?"

"Your ailing company? Yes, I have."

"And have you made a decision?"

"Not as of yet." He looked out the window, down at the pool, and his body tensed.

"I would love it if you could come to Paris for a while. See the sights, my company, take in an opera. Bring your wife if you like, or bring someone else if you need a break."

A break was exactly what he needed. Some time away. Parisian clubs and Parisian women. "Sounds like a plan, LaMont. I'll be there tomorrow. It's past time I got out of Attar."

Past time he got away from Leena, Jada and all of the ways they upended his life. Past time he took another woman to his bed and purged his system of this…this unreasonable desire for Jada. She was under his skin, and he could not allow it.

They would stay here in Attar, and he would find the man he'd always been in Paris. Alone.

CHAPTER SEVEN

"INSTRUCT THE SERVANTS on how to pack for you. We're heading to Paris in two hours."

The pronouncement seemed to shock Jada, but it shocked Alik a whole lot more. He had been planning on coming into the dining room to tell her that he would be gone for a week, and that she and Leena would stay here until his return. But that wasn't what he'd ended up saying.

"Two hours?" Jada's mouth, the mouth that he knew tasted like the most decadent dessert, rounded into a perfect O.

"Yes. I am on a time frame and you don't want to stay out here in the middle of this godforsaken desert by yourself, do you?" Frustration at himself made him sound harsher than he'd intended.

"I don't know. The alternative is going to your godforsaken bachelor pad in the middle of a French city, where you will also be—am I right?"

"You are coming with me. I am not leaving you here. It is an issue of safety."

"How is it an issue of safety? We're quite fine out here. All the modern conveniences. Light switches, even, as you pointed out."

"I do not like the idea of leaving you alone."

"Alik, you have a staff of about a hundred out here. I think we'd be fine."

"Are you honestly arguing with me about going to Paris? No woman would do that. What is wrong with you?" She made no sense to him. Trying to get out of a trip to Paris, turning down sex when she clearly wanted sex. The woman was inscrutable.

"What is wrong with me? I'm finally coming to terms with the fact that this is my life, finally finding a routine, and now you want to uproot me."

"The plan was never for you to stay here."

"I know."

"It was also the plan for you to come with me and be my date at business functions if it was required. It is now required and you will do as I tell you." He was lying. And for some reason his conscience, which until thirty seconds ago he hadn't known he possessed, twinged a bit.

"I did agree to that, Alik, you're right. But I didn't agree to submit to your every command, so you can get off your high horse and chill for a moment. If I have to be ready in two hours I'd better go figure out what I need now."

"Never mind that…I will have the servants see to it. Did you just tell me to…chill?"

"Something wrong with your hearing? I did. And you need to."

"No one talks to me that way."

"Does anyone talk to you for longer than five minutes at a time, Alik? Anyone other than Sayid, who I'd venture to say could give you a serious run for your dominance and is probably not bothered by you in the least."

"Not very many people do, and do you know why, Jada?"

She set Leena down on the floor, on her blanket and stood, arms crossed beneath her breasts. "Why, Alik? Please do enlighten me."

"Because people who are smart are afraid of me. They know that even if I'm smiling at them, I could turn on them at a moment's notice. If money passes into my hand and my allegiance is asked to be changed, it will be changed. That is why people are afraid of me. And they should be."

"I'm not afraid of you, Alik."

"I think you are."

"You think wrong."

"I don't think wrong, Jada, I know you're afraid of me. Oh, perhaps you aren't afraid of me harming you in any way, and you should not be. For all my sins, I have never hurt a woman or child, and I never would. There is a line in the sand that even I won't cross. But I think you're afraid of what might happen if I get too close. Of what might happen if I touch you. Kiss you again."

He took a step forward, watching as her pupils expanded, making her eyes appear darker, more seductive, watching her pulse throb at the base of her throat, revealing just how unnerved she was. Revealing just how turned on she was, he suspected.

"Yes, you're afraid of that," he said. "So afraid of my touch." Nearly as much as he was coming to fear hers. What it did to him. But in keeping with his character, the more dangerous something seemed, the more he wanted it.

He extended his hand, intent on cupping her cheek, feeling her silken skin beneath his fingertips and Jada jerked back like she'd seen a snake.

Jada was mainly horrified that she'd wanted to lean into his hand, that she'd longed to feel his skin against hers again. That she wanted more than what she'd gotten last night when she should really hope nothing like it ever happened again.

He was wrong, though. She wasn't afraid of him. She was afraid of herself.

"Just because I don't want it, doesn't mean I'm afraid."

"You do want it, though," he said.

"No." She bent down and scooped Leena up into her arms. "I don't. I have too much going on in my life, and frankly, so do you. We have a daughter. We have a daughter together. That means we have to be able to parent together."

"I told you, I doubt I will be doing much in the way of parenting."

"I think you will," she said, challenging him. The way he'd challenged her. "I think you're going to have to. Leena isn't an accessory to add to your home. She's not a vase that has been in your family for generations that you're owed based on lineage—she's your blood. Not a thing you hold rights to."

"It is not for my own sake that I thought to avoid her, but for hers. Don't ask why, because you know the answer."

She did. She knew why. Alik said the worst things at the worst possible times, and that was when he wasn't trying to hurt anyone. He just seemed to be missing that place inside of him that should be filled with emotion and empathy. He was void there.

The realization, the image of an empty hole in his chest where his heart should be, made her own heart feel pain. It wasn't fair. Alik had never had a chance. He had never had love or family. He'd grown into the man he was thanks to circumstances, but even though so much of it wasn't his fault, it didn't make it any less difficult for him to deal with. It didn't make it any less real.

"I know you might not know this," she said, "since you didn't know your parents, but children are able to forgive a lot of shortcomings. Because they are born loving you, trusting you. At the moment, you have that love, that trust. No matter what you say, no matter what you intend to do, no matter how distant you want to be, you will be Leena's father. And if you never try, she will have a lifetime of pain, disappointment and the breaking of that bond. Because she has that bond, Alik."

"She doesn't seem to like me," he said, looking down on Leena's head.

"She does. And she will more as she gets older. She'll love you, Alik. You will be her hero. It's how a little girl looks at her father. It's how I looked at mine. He died when I was seventeen, and it was such a shock. He'd seemed invincible to me. Superman. I always felt safe with my father around."

"How did he die?"

"My parents were older. I was a late-in-life surprise for them. I came sixteen years after their last child, my much-older brother. They were wonderful, and I didn't get enough time with them. But my father… He taught me what to expect from a man in terms of treatment, simply by treating me like a princess. I would never have settled for less, because without words he showed me what it was I deserved. You have the chance to do that for her. Or not."

"I need to go and ensure all is going as it should with the packing."

"Of course," she said.

Alik turned and walked out of the room, and a flood of emotion washed through her with such ferocity she was afraid it might bring her to her knees. She didn't feel hopeless, though, not as hopeless as she had a moment ago.

Because when Alik had turned to go she'd seen emotion in his eyes. She'd seen fear. He didn't want to let Leena down, and whether he knew it or not, he was on the road to loving her. And with that, more would follow. She had to hope so.

Right now, she just ached for him. For the man who was lost in a situation that made no sense to him. Alik was alpha, controlling and extremely capable. He had money and power, charisma to spare when he chose to apply it. But Alik didn't understand love, and in this situation, that made him infinitely more helpless and less equipped than she was.

When it came to emotion, she held the power, while he stood, defenses down, with nothing.

She kissed the top of her daughter's head and closed her eyes, repeating a promise in her mind, over and over again.

I will help your father learn to love you. Because you deserve nothing less.

She'd been on one of Alik's private planes before, but that didn't mean she was immune to the glamor of traveling in that kind of style. Not after a lifetime of flying economy. And after suffering, happily, with the inundation of luxury, brought on by having a bed available for a flight, she was completely floored by her first glimpse of Paris.

She'd been to India, with a stopover in Frankfurt,

on a visit to see her in-laws once, but beyond that, she was hardly a world traveler. Seeing so many sights in person that she'd seen immortalized in movies was a truly surreal experience.

And after being treated to her first vision of the Eiffel Tower, she was shocked even further by the location of Alik's town house. It was sleek and spare inside, the perfect foil for the view it afforded. Out one side was an alley, with a cobbled street and small, crowded shops. The patisserie, the boulangerie and various cafés with pastries guaranteed to go straight to her hips. And on the other side was the tower itself, the base of the iron structure filling the view from the kitchen windows. And from the bedrooms, you could see the rest, glittering in the darkness, iconic and surreal.

No, not even the luxury of Alik's private plane could have prepared her for it. As if a palace in Attar hadn't been sufficient to prove what sort of man Alik was, to demonstrate the sort of power he had, the opulent home in the heart of Paris drove the point home.

"Your room is here," Alik said, "Leena's is down the hall. The master is on the top floor."

"Only the master?"

"And my office, but yes."

Alik was a man of total self-indulgence. That, also, should have been clear by now. For some reason, she was understanding it slowly, in increments. Perhaps because it was so very different from the way she did things. From who she was.

She should be disgusted by his attitude. Instead, she found she was fascinated by it. Not many people were so honest about how selfish they were. Alik owned it, enjoyed it. He'd made a life that was purely for himself and he seemed happy in it.

As happy as Alik could ever be.

That thought made her sad. Reminded her that sometimes having whatever you wanted didn't add up to a satisfying life.

"So what are our plans while we're here?"

Alik put a hand in his pocket and leaned against the door frame of the bedroom. "Tomorrow night my potential client is providing us with tickets to the opera, before I meet with him the following day."

"Opera? I've never been." And she shouldn't want to go. Not with Alik. It was shockingly like a date. Because you couldn't bring a one-year-old to the opera.

"Then it shall be a culturally enriching experience for you," he said, his eyes not focused on her, but on a point somewhere past her head.

"What about Leena?"

"I have secured an au pair for the duration of our stay."

"Have you?" she asked, anger—welcome, blessed anger—spiking in her. "And what are her references? Shouldn't I have been consulted?"

"Adira took care of it, and I trust her as much as I trust anyone." She noticed he didn't say he trusted her completely. Simply as much as he trusted anyone. Because Alik didn't trust. Another piece of him to add to her puzzle. She shouldn't be working on an Alik puzzle.

No, she should be. Because she was trying to figure out how to help him have a real, positive relationship with Leena, and in order to do that she would have to understand him.

"Still, in the future, I would like to be consulted."

"Of course, my princess, whatever you desire," he said on a slow drawl, his tone mocking.

"She's my daughter. I've rarely left her alone." And she shouldn't be leaving her now. She should tell Alik no. Tell him she didn't want to go to the opera.

But she did. And it had been a long time since

she'd been out. Since she'd done something she wanted to. Something for herself.

"She will be fine. She'll be sleeping for most of the time we're gone, as she is now."

"I know," she said. "I mean, I do know but…kids make you worry."

Alik frowned. "Yes, they do. That is a universal feeling, then?"

"Yes. Everyone worries about their kids."

A slow half smile curved his mouth. "And so do I."

Even as they were preparing to leave for the opera, Alik wondered why he'd issued the invitation to her. He could have asked another woman. Could have gone to a club the night before and met someone to take out.

Better still, he could have given it a miss entirely. Opera wasn't his thing. But he had asked Jada. And he found that he actually wanted to take her.

Maybe because he was sure it was something she would never do for herself. And she looked tired, something he was certain was partly his fault.

And no matter what she'd said to him, she hadn't moved on. She was still grieving her husband; even he could see it, and he scarcely understood that emotion or any other.

That was how he found himself waiting at the base of the stairs in his town house, his heart beating a little faster than normal, waiting for her to join him. Waiting for his first sight of her in the dress he'd selected for her to wear.

That was another unusual thing. He'd never concerned himself with putting clothes on a woman before. In the past, he'd only been worried about taking them off. He was hardly a connoisseur of fashion, female or otherwise. But he'd seen the dress in a boutique window that afternoon on his way through the city and he'd known he had to have it for her.

As if on cue, he heard the sound of high heels on marble floor, and he looked up. And then it became hard to breathe. Hard to swallow.

The rich, crimson fabric made Jada's golden skin glow, the strapless, scooped neckline of the dress revealing a teasing glimpse of her full, perfect breasts. Her waist was small, the gown fitted there before gently flowing away from her hips in waves of chiffon. And when she took her first step down the stair, the fabric parted and revealed its secret, and a hint of Jada's shapely legs.

"The slit is too high," she said, walking down toward him, her hair, glossy black and wavy, shimmering beneath the lights as she moved.

"It is not high enough," he said, unable to take his eyes off her.

She stopped on the last step, the top her head still barely reaching his eyebrows. "I never wear clothes like this. It's very revealing."

"I know. And it's perfect."

"That's a very male perspective."

"I'm very male."

She blinked. "Granted."

"So then it should come as no surprise to you."

"I would love to have refused to wear it on principle, but I don't have other opera dresses lying around, and regardless of the fact that I feel like it puts far too much of me on show…I do like it." A reluctant smile tugged on the corners of her full mouth.

"I knew you would. Or rather, I knew I would, and that was all I cared about."

"So you dressed me for your own pleasure? A bit selfish, but then, that's to type I suppose."

"Feel free to enjoy me for your own selfish pleasure, Jada, if it helps."

He didn't think he imagined the slight coloring of her cheeks, the tinge of pink in her skin. She paused for a moment, her head cocked to the side, black hair sliding over her shoulder like an ink spill. "You look very nice. I've never seen you with a tie."

He raised his hand to the knot of midnight-blue silk. "It is an opera," he said, lowering it again.

"Yes, but you showed up at the courthouse in jeans."

He turned around and opened the front door. "I changed before the hearing."

"Yes, you did."

The car he'd ordered was idling outside. He put his hand up when the driver started to get out, and opened the door for Jada himself. "After you," he said.

She slid into the car and he got in after her. She was looking down, a strange expression on her face, then she looked back at him. "I haven't been on a date since...you know since when."

"Is this a date?" he asked.

Her eyes widened. "Not really, but...well, it sort of is."

"I'm not certain I've ever really been on a date," he said.

"That can't be true," she said, looking out the

window at the passing view as the car started moving. He watched where she watched, taking in the lights smearing across the darkness as they drove on. She was seeing the city for the first time. It was interesting to see it through her eyes, to see it with wonder and excitement.

"I don't date women, princess. I sleep with them."

"I see," she said, her words clipped.

"You find me crude. I understand that, but I also don't lie."

"I do appreciate that."

"But, for the purposes of tonight," he said, not understanding quite why the words rolling around in his head were giving him pleasure, only that they were, "we are on a date."

"I think I can handle that if you can."

"I have dodged enemy gunfire, and on more than one occasion, not dodged it entirely, so I think I can handle going on a date with my wife."

His words hung in the air. They'd seemed louder than anything either of them had said before. And they seemed to just float there.

He had never called her that before. Never referred to her as his wife. Because while he considered them married in the eyes of the law, he'd never thought of her with the title attached.

So maybe she was right. Maybe marriage was more than paper, even to him. But it didn't explain why he'd suddenly called her his wife.

"It's okay," she said as the car slowed. "I'll let it go if you will."

He nodded, aware that in the dim lighting she might not have seen.

The car came to a complete stop and again, he halted the driver, getting out and then rounding to Jada's side to open it for her.

He extended his hand and clasped hers in his. She felt so good, so soft and warm. And then he didn't let go. "Since we're on a date," he said, leading her up the lit, white stairs that led into the opera house.

They walked in and the lobby was filled with people, glittering from head to toe in designer gowns, tuxes and enough gems to fill the vaults of the World Bank.

Alik watched Jada's eyes as they walked through the opulent entryway. And he took notice of the high-gloss, caramel-colored marble floor, the pillars, the ceiling. Took notice of the chandelier, hanging low above them, dripping with crystals.

It had been a long time since he'd been impressed by such things. A long time since he'd even bothered to notice. When he'd been a boy, taken into the organized crime business, he'd been stunned by the glamor, by the wealth. And at some point, he had gotten used to it, and it had become tarnished by the kinds of activities he knew were often involved in the acquisition of such things.

Funny how, though he'd inhabited the world for most of this life, he had never loved it. Had never felt entirely settled in it.

Through Jada's eyes, things seemed glittery again. Strange. Interesting. And wonderful in its way.

"We're up here," he said, gesturing to the curved staircase that led away from the crowd.

"Don't tell me you have some sort of private box."

"The royal box," he said. "Actually, it's the box the last Tsar of Russia and his wife used to use when they visited Paris and got a craving for theater. It was designed specifically for them, and I think our host found himself quite clever putting me in this particular box."

"Tsar Alik. It's not so bad."

"Tsarina," he said, bowing slightly to her, gratified by the flush of pink in her golden cheeks. He took her hand in his and led her up the stairs, into the booth. A heavy velvet curtain in a robin's-egg blue was held back by thick, velvet ties. Matching curtains were tied back around the front part of the box, keeping the far recesses of it obscured to any curious onlookers.

"The thing about these sorts of boxes," he said, putting his hand low on her back and guiding her inside, "is that you don't have the best view of the stage. You are in front, which is prestigious, and if you sit in the center, you are on stage yourself. We even have our own curtain. People will look up here and wonder who we are. And that is what they're designed for."

"Very ostentatious," she said.

"Very. But it's what people do with money."

"It's not what you've done with money," she said, taking a seat in one of the plush chairs, her fingers tracing the carved wood on the edge of the arm. "You're hardly in the news, if you are at all."

"Because attention has never mattered to me," he said, taking his seat next to her.

"What does matter to you?"

It was a good question. As a kid, he had wanted to survive. To get up and live to see another day.

As an adult, he'd grown tired. Had pushed back at life, challenged it. Now that he had Leena, things had changed again. "Life to me has often just been something I was doing. I was not dead, which meant I lived, which meant I was obligated to act. I never loved my life, was never so concerned with it as some people. So I went on dangerous missions no one else would take, rode motorcycles too fast, jumped out of airplanes."

"You had a death wish, you mean?"

"Not so much. But there I was, alive. And I was trying to…feel it."

"By courting death?"

"Makes a sick sort of sense, doesn't it?"

She looked away from him, down at the filling auditorium. "Yes. It does. What is the name of the show?"

"*La Traviata.* She dies at the end."

Jada shot him a deadly glare. "Spoiler alert!"

"It's hardly a spoiler…it's opera. She always dies in the end." He leaned back in his chair, and Jada fell silent. They sat like that until the house lights dimmed, until the curtains below opened.

And the music started. And Jada was on the edge of her seat, her eyes rapt on the stage below them. While she watched the singers, he watched her, watched her shoulders tense, watched her expression contort dramatically when something would happen.

She was so beautiful to him then. So unguarded. He knew that was how people saw him. As unguarded. Perhaps he was, but it was simply because he'd never had anything to protect. He was too numb to hurt.

Jada was so soft inside. She had so much light in her, so many delicate intricacies to her that would be so simple, and so cruel to destroy. It made him worry for her. Made him feel all the more fascinated by her.

By the time intermission came, he found he could hardly breathe, and it had nothing to do with the performance happening on stage.

Jada relaxed, leaning back in her chair. "This is wonderful," she said.

"Yes," he said, his throat tight for some reason, "it is."

She stood and stretched, arching her back, her breasts rising, pushing against the fabric of the gown. Her tension might have dissipated with the halting of the production, but his had not.

He felt like something was going to burst inside of him. Like he was suddenly aware that there was a dam inside of him, a great stone wall holding back the potential for torrential destruction.

And he had to stop it. Had to shore it up with something. Something simple. Something he understood. He stood, his hand shaking, his heart thundering.

Jada looked at Alik and froze. She realized, in that moment, what it was like to be a gazelle, stalked by a predator. Except, she wasn't going to run. She didn't know why, only that she wouldn't.

The opera was mesmerizing. It was all feeling, feeling put to music, so rich and affecting. And even though she didn't understand the words, it transcended language. It went down deep inside of her, tapped into a well of emotion, a well of need, that she hadn't known was quite so immense.

And now Alik was looking at her like he wanted her. More than wanted, like he needed her. There was something dark and deadly in his eyes now. Something desperate. And she liked it, responded to it. It was different than the flat nothingness she usually saw there, different than that blasted, false, shallow front he usually put on.

In that moment, as his eyes met hers, everything fell away. Her present, her past. There was nothing but Alik, nothing but the intense, terrible ache he made her feel.

This was frightening. This was real. And it was enticing. A black flame dancing in front of her, so beautiful she couldn't look away, so dangerous she knew she had to. But she wouldn't.

Instead, she reached out her hand and prepared to touch the fire.

CHAPTER EIGHT

JADA'S FINGERS MADE contact with Alik's heated skin, and a shiver went through her body. She was burned, heat arcing through her, raging in her veins, but she wasn't hurt. And she didn't want to take her hand away. Didn't want to turn from the path she was walking down now.

And then the moment of calm was over. Alik growled, taking her into his arms and pushing her behind the curtain, against the wall. And then he was kissing her. Deep. Hard. Hungry and desperate and everything she'd ever fantasized about. Everything she'd never known to fantasize about.

"Alik," she whispered, a plea. For him to stop. For him to keep going.

He kissed her neck, her bare shoulder, his hand resting at the base of her throat, gentle, arousing. He spoke to her, low and rough, in more than one language, as if his brain couldn't settle on one in that moment. Gratifying, since she was no less confused. No less lost in the sensations that were rioting through her.

His other hand rested on her hip, his fingers curling, bunching the thin material of her dress up into his palm, widening the slit that ran up to her thigh. He brushed her bare skin with his fingers, tugged the fabric to the side.

"Alik," she said again, a warning this time.

"No talking," he said, kissing her lips.

She didn't want to talk. She wanted to kiss. So the order seemed fine enough to her. Except there was a reason she was supposed to stop him; she was sure there was. But she couldn't remember it, and even if she could, she was sure that right now she wouldn't care about it.

She just kissed him back, sucking his tongue deep into her mouth, feeding off his hunger, letting his desperation fuel her own. She tugged at the material on his suit jacket, pushed it from his shoulders.

He growled and his hand tightened at her throat, then eased, fingertips sliding down, so gentle, tracing her collarbone, curving over the swells of her breasts. She sucked in a sharp breath, her nipples puckering beneath the crimson fabric, aching for him, for his touch.

"Tell me," he said, pressing a kiss to her neck.

"Touch my breasts," she said, not sure why it was so easy to tell him what she wanted. Only that, in that moment, there was no time for embarrassment. There was no time for hesitation, for flirtation. She was on the edge of something, something she couldn't put words to, and she knew that only Alik could take her over.

Alik obeyed her command, his hands coming down to cup her, thumbs teasing her through the gown's bodice.

She tugged at his tie, loosening it, not bothering to pull the knot out completely. There wasn't time. Music swelled in the background and she didn't care. Because her need wasn't satisfied yet.

For the past three years this part of herself had been dormant. Buried. Lost. She hadn't experienced desire, hadn't burned for the touch and kiss of a man. She hadn't let herself remember what it was like, not truly.

And now she was on fire, the sensation so hot, so painful and beautiful, that she had to embrace it, had to follow the path, even if it led to total ruination. This was beyond the desire she knew. Past reason. Beyond herself.

He lowered his head and kissed the top of her

breast, his tongue tracing the line of the dress. She forked her fingers through his hair, held him there for a moment.

The hand at her hip moved, fingers teasing at the edge of her panties, dipping beneath the silken fabric, sliding through her slick folds. A low moan escaped her lips, swallowed by the music coming from below.

"You're so good at this," she said, her words broken.

He said nothing, a low chuckle vibrating against her chest as he licked and kissed his way back to her mouth, fingers pushing deeper, sliding over her clitoris. He dipped one inside of her and she bucked against him, hungry for more, hungry for everything.

She held on to the front of his dress shirt, her face buried in his chest while he worked her body with his skilled hands. An orgasm built in her, and he brought her to the edge, then pushed her away from it, his rhythm maddening, enough to turn her on more than she'd ever been in all her life, without giving her the release she craved.

"Alik, now," she said, her hands gliding down his muscular chest, to the buckle of his belt, undoing it quickly, then his pants.

He pushed them partway down his hips, freeing himself.

She took his heavy length into her hand, squeezing gently. He was a very big man, and without making comparisons, she could honestly say she'd never seen a man quite like him. But she wasn't nervous. She was too needy for that, too desperate. She knew what she wanted, and she knew he could give it to her.

He reached down and picked his coat back up, digging through the interior pocket and producing his wallet, then a condom. She could have wept with relief. At least one of them could think. She was well beyond it.

"Let me," she said, taking the packet from his hand and tearing it open, rolling it onto him quickly.

He pushed her panties to the side and put his hand on her thigh, opening her to him, positioning her. He teased her entrance with the head of his erection. The breath hissed through her teeth as he filled her slowly, completely, perfectly.

She arched into him and he slid his hand around to palm her butt, pulling her more tightly against him, pushing inside of her farther. She kissed his mouth, her hands on his back, holding on to him tightly as he thrust into her, driving them both toward completion.

She was so close, had been since he'd first touched her, but now she wanted it to last. Wanted that moment of him being in her to go on. Because it was so delicious, so incredible, far beyond her experience.

It was lust and desire, a perfect storm of physical need being met, of the need being exceeded.

He thrust deep, hard, her body pressed tightly against the wall, Alik, hot and delicious in front of her. She was surrounded by him, lost in him.

And when she reached the peak, as it built, so strong, so fast, she fought it. It was too much, too much too quickly. She was sure she couldn't survive it. It was too big, too far beyond anything she'd ever known. The sensation, the pressure, felt like too much for her body to contain, too much for her to withstand.

Then it broke over her, like a burst of stars inside, white hot and bright, overpowering, beautiful. It consumed her, burned through her like a flash fire. All she could do was cling to Alik.

She felt the moment he found his release, felt his muscles go tight, his body still, felt the shiver of pleasure that worked its way through him, the pulse of his erection deep inside her setting off a series of aftershocks.

And then she was back on earth. Back in the real world. The music didn't seem so distant, the background no longer fuzzy.

And she realized what she had done, with who and where.

"Oh no." She pushed against his chest, her hand coming up to cover her mouth.

"What?" he asked, his voice hushed.

"We just…" She looked around, tried to see if anyone was watching them. She couldn't see anyone from her position behind the curtain, only the edge of the singers on the stage, and they were completely involved in their performances. "We're in public, Alik," she hissed.

And she'd just had sex with another man. A man she didn't love. It didn't matter that he was her husband on paper because in truth, he was a stranger. If she was going to be with someone other than the man she'd loved, there had to be a better reason than blinding lust.

It made a mockery of everything she believed in. Of the values she wanted to teach her daughter. Of everything she'd always thought about herself. Of what she'd shared with the man she loved. Only with him.

And she had done it all with an audience below.

For one, terrifying moment, she felt like she was drifting without an anchor. This wasn't her. It wasn't how she was. She was sensible, she was safe. She went to bed by nine every night. She didn't have sex with strange men in opera boxes.

Tears pricked her eyes. She was horrified. She didn't want to cry in front of him, not after coming like that in his arms. It was heaping mortification on top of mortification. Because no matter how she regretted it now, there was no pretending she hadn't wanted it. That she hadn't been an equal partner, if not an instigator.

She had wanted it. That was the part that scared her most. Her body still ached, still hummed with the aftereffects of her recent release. And her frame was shaking with the effort of holding her tears at bay.

"I have to go," she said.

"The show isn't over," Alik said tightly, his eyes burning in the darkness.

"Yes, Alik. It is over," she said, not talking about the opera. "It's over for me."

She turned and swept the back curtain aside, walking out of the box and into the hall. There were people there, people milling around who could have easily walked in on them.

Her heart thundered, her legs shaking, her stomach nauseous as she made her way down the curved staircase and into the lobby, then out the front door. She ran along the line of cars idling at the curb until she found Alik's driver.

She opened the back door and the man jumped, his head rising sharply. "Mrs. Vasin?"

She didn't bother to correct him. "Yes. I need you to take me home."

"Where is Mr. Vasin?"

"He is not ready to leave yet. Take me home."

"But what about Mr.…"

"If Alik bloody Vasin is as damned resourceful as he would have me believe, then he can find his own ride home and I won't worry about him for a moment. Now take me back to the town house." She leaned back against the seat, her heart thundering.

The driver put the car into Park and started to pull away from the front of the theater. Jada looked back and saw Alik burst through the front doors, his jacket gone, his tie still loose. Then she looked at the road ahead, at the streetlights and the light reflected in the rain-covered street, and said nothing.

CHAPTER NINE

ALIK CURSED JADA AT LEAST a hundred times on his way back to his town house in his ill-gotten limousine. He'd greased the palm of a waiting driver and snagged another opera attendee's ride. He couldn't be bothered to feel bad about it.

Actually, if Jada hadn't run out on him there would be very little in the world he could be bothered to feel bad about. Not when his body was still burning with the aftereffects of his release.

Not when Jada had gone up like flame in his arms, flames that had consumed him. Damn the woman. He should have gone to a club and gotten drunk instead of following her. But for some reason he needed to be home. Needed to follow her.

Dimly, through the haze of his anger, he wondered if her kiss, her body, *had* transferred her passion to him. It was why he never should have touched her.

But it was too late for that. Much too late. The

floodgates were open and they were both going to have to deal with the consequences.

The limo pulled up to his house and he got out, slamming the door behind him and stalking into the house. He could not recall the last time he was so angry. Anger required emotion, loss of control, and both of those things were rare for him.

But now, he was in the thick of both.

He prowled up the stairs, tugging his tie off and throwing it onto the floor, then continued down the hall, his heart pounding, his body aching for more. For another taste of the woman who had brought him to heaven and then looked at him like he was the devil.

He could have caught up to her at the theater, but he'd paused at the middle of the stairs and watched her instead, watched her run out of the theater, deep crimson against the pale marble surroundings. Like a rose in the middle of stone. Triumphant, alive.

Only Jada was also angry. The emotion coming from her in waves, undeniable and somewhat awe inspiring. And then it had been as if some of it had attached itself to him, coated his skin. And then he'd felt it, too. Only he wasn't angry at himself. He was angry at her. How could she experi-

ence what they just had, the same damn thing, and
then run off?

It wasn't simply that she'd left, it was that she'd
looked like she wanted to cry. As if he'd hurt her in
some way when they both knew all he'd done was
give her pleasure. Mind-blowing pleasure at that.

He wasn't being conceited—it was the truth.

He wrenched open the door to her room without knocking and she shrieked tugging her dress
up against her breasts, attempting to cover herself.

"What the hell was the meaning of that?" he
asked, aware that he was showing his loss of control and temper, not sure that he cared.

"I might ask you the same question," she fired
back, her eyes stormy. "You just…you did that to
me in a public place. A public place! We could
have been seen. We could have been—"

And his control snapped. "I *did that* to you?" he
repeated, his voice low. "I did it. *To* you."

"Yes," she said, lifting her chin.

"Aren't you a pretty little liar. Making up sto-
ries that suit your reality. I did nothing to you. You
grabbed me. You kissed me. You were the one who
wrapped your hand around me and put the condom on, so don't you dare act the part of wounded
maiden." He advanced on her and she shrank back.

Good. Finally she saw what he was. Finally she was afraid. Just like everyone else. And he would not hold himself back, not for her, not now. Not when it was her fault that his armor was cracked, that all of this was leaking out. "If there is a part for you to play in this little opera you're conducting in your head it would be the whore, and make no mistake."

"And if I'm the whore," she spat, "what does that make you?"

"No less and no more. But I know my part, and I don't pretend to be something I'm not. I don't pretend to be above the lusts of the flesh even while I'm burning up for it."

"Have you no sense of responsibility? Of right? You act like self-control is some sort of sin, but people aren't animals and we don't just have to go around doing everything we like!"

"So proper, Jada, have you ever stepped out of line other than tonight?"

"I've never wanted to."

"You never wanted to? Or other people in your life didn't want you to?"

"What's the difference? We live for other people. At least, normal people do."

"There is a big difference, Jada. Clearly you

needed to let loose. Or tonight wouldn't have happened."

"Tonight," she bit out, "never should have happened at all. I must have been crazy to let you touch me."

"Is that right?" he asked. A new kind of heat was flowing through him now, reckless and dark. So often in his life, he felt like an observer, standing above things, watching them, manipulating, but not engaging.

He was engaged now. And the closer he got to Jada, the more tightly he embraced the anger that was pouring through him, the looser his grip on his control became.

He took a step toward her and she didn't back down, didn't shrink. Whatever moment of sanity she'd had before was gone now. Now she was ready to challenge him.

"Yes," she said, her voice thinner now, less confident, betraying the fact that, no matter how straight she stood, she wasn't as fearless as she appeared.

"Is that so, princess? You despise my touch so much?" She looked at him, stared him down, golden eyes burning. "I am so abhorrent to you?" He reached out and skimmed her cheekbone with his thumb, drawing it down to her lower lip, tracing the outer edge of her tender flesh. And he saw her react. Saw her eyes darken, her pulse flutter at the base of her throat. "Yes, clearly you could not stand to have me touch you again," he said, his tone mocking.

She jerked back from him. "I shouldn't be able to stand it," she said. "I don't know you. I don't like you, I sure as hell don't love you."

"What does love have to do with sex?" he asked.

Her mouth dropped open. "What does love have to… Sex is incredibly intimate—that I just shared it with a virtual stranger makes my skin crawl."

"There is nothing intimate about sex."

Jada thought she'd reached her limit on things Alik could say that she would find shocking. She'd been wrong. "Nothing intimate about… How can you think that?"

"Sex is just chasing release, using someone else's body to find it."

That assessment of it, of what they'd just done, was worse than anything she could have imagined. She felt used, but worse than that, she felt like a user. Like she'd pushed her pent-up sexual energy and frustration onto him, used his body to satisfy hers. Like she was no better than he was.

She shook her head, her throat closing up, her

heart pounding so hard she felt dizzy. "That's not right, Alik. It is intimate. It's important."

"How?"

"You were inside me!" she shouted, not caring if the au pair, who was installed in a room next to Leena's, could hear. Not caring if people on the street below heard. Not caring about anything but venting her anger, her frustration. Her confusion. The rage that was only directed at herself. "How is that not intimate?"

He looked frozen then, like a block of stone, his features hard, uncompromising. He was silent for a while, and when he spoke, it was like all of the color had drained from his voice. All of the anger, the frustration that had been boiling over a moment before was gone. Leaving in its place an icy calm that chilled her to her bones.

"I am not accustomed to hysterics from a woman I've just treated to so much pleasure. I would have expected a thank-you." He was using that calm, smooth voice that she was sure had seduced countless women, but beneath the words, she could hear the total detachment. Could hear them ring false.

"Why do you have to do that?" she asked.

"What?" He took a step back and leaned against the door frame.

"Why do you have to stop being angry. Stop being…anything. Why can't you just scream at me if you're mad?"

"Why can't you just admit that you want me?"

Her heart rate picked up. Why couldn't she admit it? Because it felt like a betrayal. No, not of Sunil. He was gone. She knew that, she understood it and accepted it. It felt like a betrayal of who she was. Of what she'd always believed in.

Of who she'd always thought she was. And in that, was a betrayal of her memories.

She didn't know the woman who had grabbed onto Alik's jacket, the woman who had devoured his lips like she was starving. The woman who had taken him in her hand and squeezed tight, who had urged him to take her, hard, fast and without regard to the people in the auditorium.

No, she didn't know that woman at all, and she didn't have time, or the inclination to get to know her. She had a child to raise, a dysfunctional man to try and fix so he could be a father to his daughter, and introducing her own issues into it would just mess everything up.

More than it already was.

"Because it doesn't matter," she said. "This doesn't matter. Leena matters."

"When we touch, we burn, princess. This…this isn't normal…you have to know that." His voice was low, husky. Genuine.

"I know it's not normal," she whispered. "This is as far from my normal as possible. Look at what happened tonight. I don't…I don't do this."

"You know all about sex, Jada, I can see that you do. So why does this scare you so much?"

"Because I know about sex in a committed relationship. I know about sex in bed. The wildest I've gotten is leaving the lights on. I…I never even wanted more than that. How can I want this?" The admission was torn from her and it left her feeling raw. Exposed. This whole evening had. As if a veil had been ripped away and shown the world pieces of herself she hadn't even known were there. The deepest, most secret parts of her brought to the surface for everyone to see.

"If there's one thing I know about, it's satisfying desires. If you want it, take it, Jada. There's nothing wrong with chasing a little fulfillment."

He was offering her forbidden fruit. And she wanted to take it. "Alik, it's not fulfillment. That's what you don't understand. And we can't…we can't bring this into our arrangement. I'm not like you…I can't stay detached. I can't see it as just sex, because there is no such thing as just sex to me. It means more to me than that and…I'm not going to get it from you."

He shook his head. "I won't lie to you."

"I know. I appreciate it."

He backed out the door, his hand on the knob. "I will see you tomorrow." He closed the door, leaving her to herself.

She sat on the edge of the bed and let the dress fall to the floor. She just felt numb. No, not entirely numb. She wished she could feel numb. Her body was still on an adrenaline rush from being in Alik's arms, from sparring with him. And her heart hurt from the exchange that had just happened between them.

He'd been angry. So angry. She'd never seen that depth of emotion in him before. It was encouraging in some ways that he could express it, that it existed in him. And she wondered what she'd done to bring it out.

Had she hurt him? It didn't seem possible. But if it was only sex, which was something she knew he could get anytime he wanted, why would he care if she regretted it?

She groaned and lay facedown on the bed. She

was an ass. She had told him she'd regretted being with him.

You despise my touch so much?

She'd imagined him above things like that. Above emotion. The fact that he wasn't was a comfort in some ways. In others…well, she felt like a terrible person.

A terrible, unsatisfied person who knew what she wanted, knew she shouldn't have it, and who didn't feel half as guilty about her actions tonight as she knew she ought to.

She rolled onto her back and looked at the unfamiliar ceiling. She'd uprooted her whole life for Leena. She wasn't compromising that now. Wasn't going to create an unstable environment. She had to be the rock here. Had to somehow bridge the gap between father and daughter and, at the same time, be the mother Leena deserved.

There was no time for angst about the situation with Alik. No time to sit around and self-flagellate over what she'd done tonight.

So she would push it all down deep inside of her and put a cap on it. Ignore it. And tomorrow, she would be back to normal.

There was no other option.

CHAPTER TEN

ALIK'S MEETING HADN'T gone well.

He'd gone to meet Michael LaMont with the full intention of taking on the other man's project. But he hadn't done it.

He hadn't done it because he'd uncovered some very unethical practices happening in the other man's corporation. He'd never cared about that kind of thing, not one bit. His loyalty was for sale and always had been.

But there were reports, multiple reports, of sexual harassment by executives in HR files, which he normally would never have looked at. But it had seemed important.

And as he'd been sitting there looking over the files, reading a report from an eighteen-year-old temp who had been groped repeatedly by an upper-level exec, then fired when she'd complained, he'd had one thought only: If anything like that happened to Leena when she went into the workforce, the offending hand would be removed from the man who dared touch her.

By the time LaMont had come into the office to ask Alik what he thought, Alik had very nearly shown the man, physically, what sort of mood he was in.

Instead of resorting to violence, he'd turned the job offer down flat, and had walked out. Then he'd urged the HR director to talk to the women in question about pressing charges, and promised that if the man lost his job as a result, Alik would find him work elsewhere.

He was turning into a damned altruist.

He slammed the front door of his town house, just as Jada was walking down the stairs with Leena on her hip. His heart, which seemed to be doing a lot more than pumping blood through his body lately, jumped into his throat.

It was very different than when she'd come down the stairs the night before. Her hair was tied back in a ponytail, a simple T-shirt covering her curves, a pair of gray track pants riding low on her hips, disguising the shape of her legs.

He regretted he hadn't seen her naked. If he had, he probably wouldn't feel the need to stare at her like this. He probably wouldn't still burn for her. And his heart probably wouldn't be in his throat.

He couldn't remember feeling curious about a woman after sex. Couldn't remember feeling drawn to her in a particular way. His sexual relationships were brief and mutually beneficial. One woman wasn't more important than the one that came before, or the one that would come after.

So the fact that he'd had sex with Jada, but hadn't seen her body, must be responsible for the lingering feeling of the unfinished.

That and the fact that she'd been the first woman to end things with him. There hadn't even been things to end. A brief screw against the wall and she'd run like Cinderella at midnight. Then when he'd found her, she'd made it abundantly clear that she never wanted him to touch her again.

Rejection on that scale was unheard of for him, and he found he didn't like it. He didn't even find it tolerable. And the memory of the rejection, combined with his current mood, was starting to feel a bit deadly.

"Good afternoon," she said, her tone a touch too bright. "Lunch is just about to be served on the patio. I didn't know if you would be home, but just in case, I had a setting put out for you."

She whisked past him and toward the back of the house.

He followed, unsure of what to think. Now she'd succeeded in putting him on his back foot twice in less than twenty-four hours. He didn't like that, either.

The little fenced-in patio that sat behind the house was, in fact, prepared for lunch. Ham and mushroom feuillités, macaroons and café au laits were spread out on the bistro table. There was also a plate of fruit and a high chair for Leena.

"You have taken over as mistress of the house, I see," he said, taking a seat and a bite of feuillité.

"I am your wife for all intents and purposes, Alik, and we are attempting to be a family. That means I should be at home in your homes, right?"

"I suppose," he said. He hadn't thought much about it before. Not initially. Because he had thought of them as guests in his home, a home that he wouldn't be in. Now things were becoming complicated. More tangled together.

He found that, for some reason he no longer saw it as sufficient to simply leave Leena in a luxury home to be provided for monetarily. Perhaps that was because of what Jada had said to him about fathers. About her father.

He'd never had one, not that he'd known, so had no idea the function a father could serve. But he did know that he didn't want his daughter growing up to be like him.

"Yes," he said, this time firmer, more sure, "it is right that you should take over that position. And also, I wanted to talk to you about living arrangements."

"What about them?"

"We must live together. I do travel a lot, and when I'm on short-term trips staying in hotels, I imagine Leena would find it more stable to stay at home. But when I am on a long-term business trip, for more than a month, or when I change residence for part of the year I would like you both to come with me."

Jada's eyes widened as she finished buckling Leena in her high chair and took a seat across from him. "Really? And what about your…social life?"

She meant women. He could tell by the frost in her tone. He didn't know why, but he found her jealousy gratifying. "I will find a way to manage it discreetly. It will not be a problem for either of you."

"I see." She looked down into her coffee. "What made you change your mind?"

"What you said the other day about your father. About all the difference he made to you. About how his presence taught you what sort of treatment to expect." He looked at Leena, so small and innocent, her cheeks round. And she looked at him, a smile spreading over her face. He'd never really paused to look at her before. Not once in the past few weeks. Not closely.

Now that he did, he felt like his chest was too full. Like his heart would be crushed with the pressure building there.

"I would not want Leena to choose a man like me," he said. He thought back to the reports he'd seen today. No, he'd never been the sort of man to press unwanted advances on a woman, but he still felt disturbed by it all. By the thought of Leena as a woman who would have to go out in the world and deal with men who wanted to hurt her. Or even men who didn't want to hurt her, but might, as they used her for their own selfish ends.

"I wouldn't want to teach her to expect that the man in her life should be absent, that he should be concerned with his own well-being, rather than hers. I would not want her to believe that she should accept money and physical comfort over love."

"Alik…you can give her more than you think. I know you can."

"I don't know it," he said, the pressure in his chest growing stronger, more unbearable. "I know what she should have. I know what's important. I see it, I understand it, but I don't know how to feel it."

"That's not true, Alik. I think you feel more than you let yourself."

"Such confidence in a man you don't want touching you," he bit out.

She looked down. "How was your meeting?"

"Neatly done, Jada. And my meeting was unsuccessful. I turned him down."

"Why?"

"I can't work for a man like him. I don't know why. Only that I can't."

She looked up at him, golden eyes shimmering. "I know why."

"Enlighten me."

"Because you do feel."

"Is that what you call this?"

"You're already changing, Alik. Two weeks ago you wanted to drop us off in Paris and never see her. Two weeks ago you thought she needed a nanny, not a mother. And now you see the difference. Now you see what she needs."

"I still have no idea what I'm doing."

"I don't, either. Still, caring, even if it's confusing, has to be better than spending two weeks with Leena and not changing the way you feel about her."

"All I know is that I want her to have everything, and I fear I don't have the ability to give it to her."

"All parents feel that way," she said, reaching across the table and putting her hand over his. A comforting touch. Not sexual, which was the only way he was used to being touched by women. Not violent, which was the only way he'd ever been touched by men.

He couldn't recall ever receiving comfort from another person before. Two weeks ago he would have said he didn't need it. In this moment, he felt like he did.

Perhaps he was changing. And he had no idea what that might mean. For the future, for the way he handled his life.

"Then I suppose I'm partway to the point I need to be."

"Worrying?"

He nodded. "I've never worried much," he said.

"Because in my experience, worry fixes nothing. When I was starving, worrying about where food would come from wouldn't deliver it to me—it required action. Worry wouldn't serve me on the battlefield—it would distract me. And yet I find with her...I worry."

Emotion was coming easier these days. Odd, after a life spent chasing feeling, it would come so suddenly now. Anger with Jada. Rage at LaMont. Worry for Leena.

"You worry because you care, don't you?" he asked, looking at Leena again, watching her attempting to pick up a slippery piece of melon.

"Yes, Alik," Jada said, her voice choked. He looked at her then, at the moisture glistening in her eyes. "That's why you worry."

Jade closed the door to Leena's room and let out a long breath. Leena hadn't been that nasty about going to bed in a long time. But tonight, she'd been more interested in gripping the crib rails and bouncing on the mattress than she'd been in sleeping.

And the mostly adorable hyperactivity had turned into wailing when Jada had shut off the light and insisted it was time to settle down. All attempts at rocking and singing had been resisted bitterly.

But her wailing had eventually turned to whimpering, which had turned into reluctant sleep. And Jada was now way past ready for bed and on her way to whimpering too.

She started down the hall and stopped when she saw a dark shadow separate from the wall and start moving toward her.

"Alik?"

"She was upset?"

"Just having a princess fit because she didn't want to go to sleep, that's all."

She could see the tension leave his silhouette. He drew closer, a shaft of moonlight coming in from outside illuminating him. Shirtless, a pair of athletic pants low on his hips. He was a beautiful man.

Beautiful, rough, broken. And he called to her. Made her heart beat fast, made her body ache. She'd been intimate with him—no matter what he might want to call it—and she knew him now. Her body knew his.

Though, she didn't feel like she'd explored him enough. Not to the degree she wanted to.

And you won't.

Stern, sensible Jada chimed in, the voice of reason. Which was a nice thing to have on hand because her body wasn't in a reasonable place. Her body was just remembering how it had felt to be near him, to have him kiss her, to have him take her to the peak and push them both over the edge.

She blinked. "You couldn't sleep?"

"I was concerned."

"Why didn't you come into the room?"

He lifted one shoulder, a casual gesture, but she knew him well enough by now to know it was anything but casual. Alik feeling concern for another person wasn't usual, or casual. "I didn't feel it was my place."

"Of course it's your place, Alik. You're her father."

He nodded slowly then lifted his arm, drew his hand over his hair and let out a sigh. "I feel like you have something with her. That you understand things I do not."

"You aren't the only one to feel that way."

"You make me feel almost normal," he said, his tone dry.

"Nobody feels like they know what they're doing with their own kids, Alik. We just sort of hope for the best."

"Even you?"

"Yes. Even me. Especially me. Deciding to adopt while I was single was something I struggled with. Because I always believed that a child should have a mother and father."

"Why didn't you and your husband have any children?"

Jada still felt protective of Sunil when it came to that subject. His family had started asking when they would start having children from the moment they'd gotten married and hadn't let up until his death.

She'd never told them, never told anyone why in their six years of marriage they hadn't managed to conceive. It had hit at his pride. That he could pro- vide for her financially, but couldn't give her some- thing she wanted so badly had been the source of so much pain for him.

No matter what she'd said, he could never really believe that she didn't resent it. And eventually, he hadn't wanted to talk about it at all.

"We couldn't," she said. "We couldn't have chil- dren. I mean…he couldn't. But we were married and that made it *us* who couldn't."

"And you decided not to pursue artificial means of conception?"

Jada almost laughed. Leave it to Alik to ask the

most personal, inappropriate questions and not have a clue he was being personal or inappropriate. "My husband wasn't comfortable with the idea of me carrying another man's baby. And frankly, he wasn't all that interested in the adoption idea, either."

"Even though you wanted children?"

"He did, too. But…but he hadn't worked through the disappointment of the fact that it wouldn't happen for us the way he'd imagined. He took it personally."

"See what emotion gets you? Logically, he should have just made sure you could have the children you wanted regardless of how."

"You say that, Alik, but even you were all about the blood connection."

"I know. But I see…I see now that it's not the blood connection that builds the strongest bond. You…you effortlessly connect with her and I struggle."

"But you do connect. You have."

He nodded slowly. "I turned down working with LaMont because he was covering up the fact that one of his top execs is sexually harassing female employees. And all I could think of was that if some man did that to Leena I would…I fear I would kill them, Jada, and I don't mean that figuratively. I would. I could."

"Alik…"

"Emotion…it is not logical. It is inconvenient. It makes it almost impossible to…live with myself."

He let out a sound somewhere between a groan and a growl and leaned against the wall, his head tilted back. He needed something. Emotional comfort, emotional connection, and she knew he would never allow it. Would never recognize it.

She wanted to give it. Wanted to tell him everything would be okay. She wanted to…

What she wanted to do, what she really wanted, was to touch him. Because he understood the physical. He understood touch and sex. It was how he connected. She wanted to cut through the confusion and give him something familiar. And at the same time, she didn't want to be familiar. Didn't want to be just another body.

She wanted to reach him. To help him.

If she was really honest—really, really honest—she just wanted to touch him.

But she wasn't going to be honest, because honesty might stop her. And she didn't want to stop.

This could be okay. If she kept it separate from

emotion, like he did. Kept it separate from marriage, then it might be okay.

She took a step toward him and put her fingertips on his chest, on the start of his tattoo, the one over his heart. The one he'd gotten before he'd risked his life to rescue his friend, the man he thought of as a brother.

His hand shot up and caught her arm, held it away from his body. "Be careful," he bit out. "Because I swear if you touch me again, I will have you naked and in my bed before you can protest."

"I'm not going to protest so you won't be able to test the theory." She said it with a lot more boldness than she felt, but she realized that she'd made the decision the moment she'd taken a step toward him.

She wanted him again. If they left it at the night at the opera, it would never truly be over. It had been too fast. Too intense. A memory that was scorched around the edges, covering it all in the hazy smoke of fantasy. There was no way it had been as good as she remembered. No way it had been so all-consuming, so soul-destroying.

She lifted her other hand and cupped his cheek, sliding her thumb over the rough shadow of stubble that covered his jaw. "I want you," she said.

"Really?" he bit out. "Because I seem to recall you running from me as though I had forced you the last time you begged me to touch you. I wasn't a fan of that."

"I'm not going to run this time," she said, her voice trembling. Even as she said it, she wasn't sure she could keep her promise.

Because the closer she got to Alik, the less hazy her memory became. The longer she left her palm on his face, against the heat of his skin, the more he burned into her. And she was shaking, terrified that being with him again would reduce her entirely to ash. She was shaking, afraid of what she felt. Of what she intended to do.

But she couldn't turn back, either.

"Promise," he said, leaning in, his lips skimming her cheek. He nipped her ear, lightly, leaving behind a light sting that he soothed with the tip of his tongue. "Promise me," he repeated.

"I promise," she said.

"Tell me you want me."

"I want you, Alik."

It was enough for him. It must have been. He pulled her up against his chest, kissing her hard, deep. She wrapped her arms around his neck and held him to her, kissing him back, matching his desperation, his hunger.

The beast he woke up inside of her was something she'd never known about before. The desire, the need, from a part of her she hadn't been aware existed.

She knew about desire, she knew about pleasure, but this…this was new. This need that verged on pain, this hunger that bordered on insanity. She felt like he was air, like having him was essential, something she couldn't live without.

It made it impossible for her to think. And that thoughtlessness was bliss.

"Bedroom," she panted as he kissed down her throat, his teeth scraping her collarbone.

"Mine or yours."

"Whichever is closer."

"Yours," he said, picking her up and carrying her down the hall. She wrapped her arms around his neck, awed by his strength, which, she was sure, was the reason he'd done it. That and to make her feel tiny and feminine. Both had worked.

He pushed the bedroom door open and set her down, then slammed it shut behind them. He flicked the light on, a wicked grin on his face.

"What?" she asked. "Why did you turn the lights on?"

"Didn't you say that you've had sex with the lights on?"

"Yes, but…" Just not quite so purposefully.

"I want to see you," he said, pushing his pants down his narrow hips. "It's a priority this time around."

Her jaw slackened a little bit when he was naked in front of her. Completely. She'd seen most of him, but not all of him at one time. He was utter masculine perfection, hard-cut lines of muscle, deep scars that were marring his skin, a map of his life, marks that had been inflicted on him by those who had meant him harm.

And the ink on his skin, marks he'd chosen for himself.

"They say men are visual," she said, "but I'm feeling pretty visual myself right now."

"As am I," he said, skipping over the compliment. "Show yourself to me."

Her breath shortened, became labored. It was such a strange way to put it. Evidence of the fact that English wasn't his first language. But it meant more this way, too. She was showing herself to him.

A part of herself she had never seen or known

about. A part no one had ever seen or known about. Deeper. More sensual. The only question was if she was brave enough. Not simply to uncover it for him, but to reveal it to herself.

Maybe if she'd had a choice, she wouldn't have done it. But there was no choice. This thing, this desire, it was bigger than she was. And tonight, it won over everything else. Over reserve, over fear.

She slowly peeled her top over her head, leaving her breasts bare for him. She shivered, nerves and the chill in the air raising goose bumps on her skin, arousal making her nipples pucker.

She pushed her pants down her legs, and her panties with them. "Just for you," she said. And she meant it. This part of her, this woman who would make love in a box at the opera, she was just for Alik. Somehow, he made her different.

Later, she would worry about it. She might even regret it. But not now.

"I am a lucky man." He crossed to her, cupping her cheek, the gesture tender, at odds with the heat and intent burning in his eyes.

She wrapped her arms around his neck and pulled his body against hers, pulled him in for a kiss. Skin to skin. She needed it. Needed him, his touch. Needed him to push her past the point of reason, past the point of thought.

He'd done it before, with such ease, and she needed it again.

He gripped her thighs and lifted her so that her legs were wrapped around his waist and he was supporting all of her weight. It brought the heart of her against the hard ridge of his erection, sending a spark of pleasure through her, deep and all-consuming.

And she was there. Beyond thought. Beyond anything other than feeling.

He kissed her neck, whispered things in her ear. Husky, dark words. Some she understood, some she didn't, but the intent didn't need translation.

"Take me," she whispered, broken, needy. Alik would fix her. He would answer the ache inside of her body. The one that went deeper than the physical.

He lay down on the bed, bringing her down on top of him. She started to adjust her position, to take him inside of her body. His hands tightened at her hips. "Stop."

"What?" she panted.

"Condom."

"Where?" she asked.

"Drawer."

"Oh." She hadn't looked in her nightstand drawer since arriving in Paris. And there they were. She might feel weird about it later, might feel bad that Alik had protection everywhere, because clearly he was the sort of man who did what he wished when the mood hit. But for now, she was just grateful.

She handed the protection to him and he applied it, then she moved back where she'd been and lowered herself onto him. Slowly, as slowly as she could manage, enjoying the tease. Enjoying the pained look on his face.

She liked that she had the power to torture him. To make him sweat and shake. It made her feel strong. It made her feel beautiful. Like a woman. A woman who was enough for the man she was with. A man who felt no inhibition, no issues with himself or who he was, or his ability to satisfy her.

Being with Alik was like waking up. Like bursting through the surface of the water after being under for too long. She hadn't even realized she was suffocating.

He gripped her hips tightly, thrust up inside of her. Her head fell back and she put her hands on his shoulders, rode him, found the rhythm that worked for both of them.

She looked down at Alik's face, the intensity, the focus. She bent down and kissed his mouth, sliding her tongue against his and he stiffened beneath her, shuddering out his orgasm. He swore and turned her over, reversing their positions and then pressing a kiss to her breasts, sucking on a nipple deep inside his mouth, continuing down her body.

He gripped her legs and hooked them over his shoulders, gripping her buttocks tight in his palms and pulling her up to his mouth, burying his face between her thighs before she had a chance to catch her breath.

"Alik…" She shuddered, his tongue tracing a streak of fire over her damp flesh.

He pushed two fingers inside of her, working them in time with his lips and tongue, pushing her higher, farther than she imagined possible.

Nothing had ever felt this good. Ever. Alik knew her body, knew just what she needed. Knew when she needed more, knew when to bring her down just so he could push her back to the edge again.

He kept it going until she was sure she would die from the pleasure. She opened her mouth to beg him to stop, to beg him to end it and let her come, but the words died on her lips, incoherent moans taking their place.

Still holding her lower body tightly with one hand, he took his other hand and reached up, pinched her nipple lightly between his thumb and forefinger while continuing his sensual torture with his mouth and she broke completely, shattering into a thousand, glimmering pieces. She wasn't sure she would ever be whole again, and she wasn't sure she cared.

She was lost in the pleasure, in the release that kept coming, wave after wave, so big, so intense she didn't know if she could withstand it. He kept tasting her, kept sliding his tongue over her damp skin until she shook, until her body was racked by tiny tremors, aftershocks of the release that had undone her completely.

And when it was over, Alik was there. And she wanted to run. But she'd promised she wouldn't. So she lay there instead, shaking.

Alik rose up and kissed her lips, his skin damp with sweat and her own arousal. He sat on the edge of the bed, his expression flat. "I don't know what happened," he said.

"You don't…"

"Usually I am more considerate than that. I lost my control for a moment. It won't happen again. Good night, Jada." He sat straight for a moment, indecision flashing across his face, then he leaned in and kissed her again. "I'll see you in the morning."

He got up and walked out of the room.

Jada hadn't run. But Alik had.

CHAPTER ELEVEN

ALIK DID HIS BEST TO WASH the impression of Jada from his skin with a cold shower. When that didn't work, he went for a run, hoping the rain and a bit of physical punishment would take care of things for him.

It didn't. By the time he collapsed in his bed, the sky was turning gray, the sun rising up behind the clouds.

He growled and got back out of bed, stalking down to the kitchen. His cook had just gotten in. He gave terse orders in French for her to prepare breakfast to be served out on the patio again. He wanted to eat out there like they'd done yesterday morning. Like they'd done before Jada had stripped his skin from his bones, left him feeling raw and exposed.

It was because he'd come before she had. That had to be it. He hadn't been that quick on the draw since he'd been a teenager. But damned if he could have stopped himself. And that was just far too telling.

He had never considered himself a man who held control in high esteem. He did what he wanted, when he wanted to do it. Some had called him debauched, and they weren't that far off. There were years of his life that he could barely remember, and it wasn't for any good or honorable reason.

Now he wondered how much of himself he'd truly kept bound up. How much of that sense of emotionless came from control. How much he had inflicted on himself. Because what had happened with Jada disturbed him, and it was beyond a simple matter of male pride.

"I thought I heard you growling down here." He turned and saw Jada behind him, in the clothes she'd been wearing the night before. Clothes she'd stripped off for his pleasure.

"I am not growling."

"You most certainly were. I could hear a rumbling coming from down here and no distinct words."

"I didn't sleep well last night."

"Join the club."

She was angry, he could tell. Not shooting sparks at him with her eyes, but definitely angry.

"Where is Leena?"

"Sleeping. Like a sane person. It's barely five o'clock."

"And why are you up?"

"The same reason you are, I imagine."

"We aren't going to have a heart-to-heart, Jada. Something like that requires both parties have a heart."

She stalked forward and fisted his T-shirt in her hands, tugging hard. And he followed the direction of the pull. She pressed her mouth to his, took his lower lip between her teeth and nipped him lightly. Then she released him.

"You can't run from that, Alik. I tried it already, remember?"

"Yes, Jada, I remember. And I don't run. I've withstood artillery fire…I'm hardly backing down from a woman who barely comes up to the center of my chest."

"Yeah, yeah. I keep hearing about all that. Big Bad Alik Vasin. But you ran last night."

"I don't spend the night with women I…" The look on her face forced him to swallow the last crude word he'd been about to say. "I'm not the kind of guy who cuddles after."

"Fine," she said, so clearly not fine it was almost comical. "But it would be nice if you stayed for more than five seconds. I know I'm not your wife. Well, I am, but you know what I mean. We aren't in love. The vows we took…we didn't mean them. I know that. I know someday you're going to get tired of me and go back to doing what it is you do with women." She took a deep breath. "I'm not your real wife. I'm also not some bimbo you picked up at a club."

"I know that."

"I don't think you do," she said. "Because you treated me like one last night. You left so fast it made my head spin. I'm not experienced at this. I've only been with one other man and not until after I married him."

"You are married to me," he said, "whether or not you love me."

She sighed. "I suppose. But the point is, this whole sexual thing…I'm not sure what to do with it. I'm not sure how I feel and the last thing I need is for you to confirm what I'm afraid is true."

"And that is?"

"Am I…is something wrong with me that I want this? That I don't care if I love you, or if I even like you?"

"Sex doesn't have to be connected to feelings,

princess. In my experience it never has been. Sex is your body."

"My body wants things that are bad for me. All the time. Take chocolate cake for example," she said. "I love chocolate cake. With lots of frosting. And I would eat it all the time. I crave it. If I listened to my body I would be eating chocolate cake for breakfast today, but just because I want it doesn't mean I should have it."

"But that's half of what makes it so good," he said, for his own benefit more than hers.

Maybe that was all it was. Maybe that was part of the excitement of being with her. She was the last woman he should want. She was his wife, but he didn't intend to make her his actual wife. Being with her like this was complicated and messy and bad.

Perhaps that was why his body responded so enthusiastically to it.

"It's human nature," he said. "To want the one thing you shouldn't have. Forbidden fruit is sweeter."

"Is that what this is?"

"Would you dislike it so much if it was?"

"I'm confused by it. I've always done what I should. I've always liked doing the right thing.

But…what did it get me, Alik? What did it get me but hurt in the end? If I would have kept playing by the rules I would have lost Leena, too."

"So play dangerous for a while, Jada. Play with me." This he could do…this was easy. It certainly wasn't anything new or different. A little bit of harmless sex. He'd overreacted. He could see that now.

"What about when it ends? It might be difficult."

"Would it be any easier to stop now?" he asked.

She shook her head. "No. I don't want to stop now."

"You like living a little dangerously, don't you?"

The color in her cheeks deepened. "Yes."

"I thought you would."

He advanced on her, intent on tasting her lips again. Leena's sharp cry, carrying all the way down the stairs, made him stop.

"Sorry," she said. "I have to get her."

He wanted to go, too, he realized. But she didn't need him. And he didn't want to interrupt her. So he shoved it aside. It wasn't important.

"I will see that breakfast gets laid out for everyone. A banana, for Leena, am I right?"

"Her favorite."

He nodded. "Then I will make sure she has it."

* * *

Jada lay back on the bed, utterly spent. She could hardly catch her breath. Alik was a ruthless lover. He made her beg. He made her scream. And she had no complaints.

She wanted to ask him to stay, but she really didn't want to sound needy. Even though she felt needy. She didn't want him to know.

He kissed her and she clung to him, still hungry for him. Maybe she could tempt him to stay with the promise of more sex. He certainly wasn't going to stay and cuddle. He'd made that very clear and he'd kept that promise for six nights running.

Things were certainly hot between them. They were officially having a physical-only affair. She cared for him, yes. As the father of her daughter. But it was nothing truly personal to her.

You are such a liar.

But, very true to what he'd said at the beginning of their marriage—when had she started to think of it that way?—he seemed to keep sex and what happened during the day completely separate. And that did bother her a little. She was all for separate but he took it to a ridiculous degree.

Except for those moments when their eyes would lock. Over the table at breakfast, when they were passing in the hall, and the fire between them would burn so hot, so bright that it was a miracle they didn't just sweep everything aside and tear each other's clothes off.

They saved that passion for the nights. Half the night, anyway. And then Alik left. Went back to his room. To his own space.

"Alik?" She settled beneath the covers, searching for a topic to delay him. "Tell me more about how…how you're here."

"You know where babies come from, I assume. You just proved you know it proficiently well, actually." He arched one brow. "And that you're also well versed in bedroom activities that don't make babies."

"That's not what I meant," she said, determined not to be offended by his ridiculousness. He *wanted* her offended. She knew him well enough to realize that. A week ago, she probably *would* have been offended. For some reason, she just wasn't now. "You were an orphan in Moscow."

"Yes," he said. "In one of the very overcrowded children's homes. You've never seen anything like that, Jada. Cribs in rows with narrow walkways for the workers to get through. Maybe three people trying to manage all those children. Someone is always crying. And when it gets terribly over-crowded, the older children have to go."

Jada closed her eyes. "Oh no…"

"I was twelve, older than some. Lucky, really. Because while the orphanages are overcrowded and understaffed, they try. They aren't cruel. It's not love or affection, but food and shelter go a long way in helping make a child's life bearable. After that there was nothing. I was lucky, I avoided having to sell my body. I found I had a talent for theft and manipulation. Which, as I told you, caught the attention of the local organized crime family."

He sat back down on the edge of the bed, still naked. "And for them, I did errands. Small things, delivering packages with unknown contents. And then I would also strategize heists. Big heists. And I thought it was brilliant. Here I was fourteen, fifteen years old and I was the criminal mastermind behind some of Europe's most notorious burglaries. Not a bad achievement for a kid with nothing. But ultimately, at some point, I had to face the reality that I was doing work for the Mob and to be honest, morally bankrupt bastard that I am, not even I cared much for that."

"And then what did you do?"

"Disappeared. Which you have to do for a while

in my position. I went into Asia. Lived in Singapore, then Japan. Tended bar, ran petty scams, did a lot of things the United States Surgeon General would advise against."

"And you were in Japan when that man approached you to help a militia strategize a government takeover."

He nodded slowly. "You listen well."

"You're interesting."

"Is that what you call it? Interesting. Perhaps I am. But I find very little to be proud of in my past. There's nothing hard about following the money. You don't have to decide what you think is right or wrong. You sell yourself to the highest bidder. Whoever has the money is right. So simple. So perfect. So very easy."

"I'm sure you weren't so bad, Alik."

"I put missions in motion that cost men their lives and to this day, I don't know what every cause I stood with was. I only knew they paid me. And I knew that the thrill of danger made me feel alive. It was only when I met Sayid that I got caught up in the rights and freedom of a nation. Attar was under attack by neighboring factions and Sayid hired me to help wipe them out. They were terrible people, Jada, and I saw the kinds of things they were doing. And then I saw Sayid risk himself, his men, everything, to save the life of a woman. And I realized I would not have done the same. Sayid got himself captured, and I was free. I didn't deserve freedom, not when men of Sayid's caliber rotted in jail. So I made it my mission to free them. There was no money involved in that. It was the first decision I had ever made in my life that was for someone else, and not for me."

"You're a good man, Alik."

He shook his head. "It took a good man to show me just how far gone I was. But I have changed. Now I'm just a corporate killer." He shook his head and stood. "And that's my story, Jada."

"It's not over yet. And you did something different here. You turned down working for a corporation that violated your ethics. To appease a conscience I know you have."

"Whatever I have, whatever I feel…it's because of Leena."

"That's how it should be. It's the same for me. She…she saved my life." *And so did you.* The words hovered on the tip of her tongue, but she held them back. She only looked at him. Because she wasn't sure if they were true. Alik had torn her from her comfort zone. Taken her from friends, from the life she knew, from everyone who had an expectation of her and left her feeling like she was drifting out at sea. Free. Terrifying.

"Do you want to know what this says?" he asked, lifting his arm and exposing the words written in ink beneath.

"What?"

"Little thieves are hanged. Great thieves escape." He lowered his arm. "I was a great thief. And I escaped. I was young and cocky, so I had this tattooed on my body to let the world know that it was my greatness that would keep me from getting caught. But you know what? You can't escape your past. I escaped arrest. I was never killed by an enemy. But my past remains, and I am trapped in it. A creation of it. So you see, no thief escapes, princess. Not even me."

She touched his bicep, her fingers drifting over the muscle. "Will you punish yourself forever?" *Will you?*

Again, she ignored her own thoughts.

"I don't have to. I don't seek to punish myself, but you asked what made me, and the simple fact is, it was nothing good that had a hand in my creation. What I am simply is. It's not me punishing myself, or the world punishing me. But my existence is a consequence for everything that has come before. There's no changing it."

She had seen Alik angry. She'd seen him totally out of his depth. She'd seen tenderness, deeply hidden but evident, when he looked at Leena. But she'd never heard him sound hopeless. Tonight, he sounded hopeless. He sounded like he wanted more than what he was.

And it broke her. Because he didn't see what she did. He didn't see what he could be. But he did want more. He was changing. And he was capable of change, no matter what he thought.

He turned to go and her heart slammed hard against her breastbone. She craved him. By her side, in her bed, her arms. No matter what he'd done, no matter where he'd been.

This dangerous, difficult, damaged man.

She wanted to reach out, to offer comfort. To take comfort. But she was too raw. She needed distance, too. Needed escape.

So she let him go. Because the alternative was calling him back and further cementing a bond that she couldn't handle.

CHAPTER TWELVE

"WE NEED TO TAKE LEENA OUT," Alik said, the next morning at breakfast. "She hasn't been anywhere except the back patio the whole time we've been in Paris."

"*I've* barely been anywhere but the back patio," Jada said, lifting her mug to her lips and leaning back in her chair, soaking in the early-morning window of sunshine that filtered through the trees, casting spots of light and shadow onto the brick floor.

"Liar, you walk to the Eiffel Tower every morning."

"And I bring Leena with me."

"Still, I think… It seems she hasn't been out enough."

For a moment, the strangeness of it all hit her full force. She was in Paris, had been for a few weeks, sleeping with a man she'd only just met. Married to the man. And the things she did with him…the things she wanted from him.

Just thinking of it made her hands shake.

She looked down at her hands, trying to orient her thoughts. And she realized she hadn't put Sunil's ring on her right hand that morning. She'd put on the rings Alik had given her, but nothing else.

She looked back up at him. "You want us all to go out together," she said, realizing slowly that that's what was happening. That he didn't know how to articulate it, or didn't want to. She wondered if he was having the same, surreal moment she was.

"That seems…normal."

"It is."

He nodded once, sharply, as though he'd known, the whole time, that his request was perfectly normal. The thing was, she imagined he didn't. He had no reference for what families did. Nothing beyond what was in movies or TV. And Alik didn't seem like the kind of man who curled up on his couch at night for prime-time sitcoms.

Even if he had, they were hardly scripted television. Nothing about their situation followed a logical path.

"Then, let's go out. What would you like to do?" she asked.

He shrugged. "I don't know."

"You must know, Alik." It came out shorter than she'd intended, but she was feeling edgy. And her right hand felt bare. More exposed skin. Less to hide behind.

"I don't."

"You don't have any ideas?" She didn't believe him. But it was also obvious that he wasn't willing to share his thoughts with her.

"We could just walk," he said, "and see where we end up."

She accepted his evasiveness. Mainly because she was too caught up in her own thoughts. In her own fears of exposure. "That sounds good to me."

"She's getting tired of the stroller," Jada said, looking down at Leena, who was wiggling and pushing against her restraints.

They stopped and Alik looked down at her, frowning. "I suppose I could hold her. But she didn't like it the last time I did that."

"More than three weeks ago, Alik."

That made his frown deepen. "Oh." He bent then, swift and decisive, and freed Leena from her seat, pulling her up into his arms.

Leena's fist curled around his shirt collar, her

other hand going to the hair on the back of his neck. He grimaced when she tugged, but he didn't reprimand her.

"All right, let's keep walking," he said.

She didn't say anything as they kept walking down the busy streets, she just kept watching Alik when she was sure he wasn't looking at her. His hold on Leena was strong, but gentle. His eyes were on their surroundings, not on his daughter.

They went through a narrow alley with cobble-stones and bistro tables. People were sitting and chatting, drinking coffee and eating pastries, both of which looked like a good idea to Jada, but Alik definitely had another agenda. One he still wasn't sharing. Which left Jada alone with her thoughts. At the moment that wasn't necessarily a good thing because her thoughts were edgy and confused.

They passed through the alley and back out onto a busy main street, walking in the opposite direction they had been now.

"Are we going back already?" she asked.

"Back to the tower."

"Oh."

They crossed back through the web of streets, in the direction of the town house, cutting through an open-air market filled with flowers, racks of books and fruit. Alik didn't spare the sights a second glance. So very typical of him. He could be so focused on whatever his internal mission was, on getting from point A to point B, that he didn't look at the beauty that surrounded him.

And you've been so different the past few years? You've had blinders on.

Alik stopped then at a carousel, one she passed every morning, stationed out in front of the tower, enticing tourists to spend money with bright colors, glittering gems and music that sounded like it was coming from a jewelry box.

"This is where you wanted to go the whole time, isn't it?" she asked.

He shrugged. "I had thought she might like it."

"She's a little small to go by herself," she said. "But I—" she looked at Alik, at Leena, grinning in his arms "—you could take her."

"I could?"

"Yes. You could. She'll be fine. Look, she's happy with you."

He looked down at Leena and swallowed. "All right."

He approached the man who was running the carousel and spoke to him in French, explaining the situation, Jada assumed. That was one thing about Alik, he might seem out of his element with a baby in his arms, but as a traveler, he was the man you wanted with you. He knew customs, and languages, knew where to go and what to order at restaurants. He knew opera.

There was no end to the general knowledge the man possessed. Not only that, but he'd been shot, had crossed enemy lines, had broken into a horrible prison to rescue his friend.

But put a baby in his arms and he looked like a man scared for his very life.

A curious man, her Alik.

She blinked. When had she started thinking of him that way? When had he become hers? She looked away from him, looked at tourists, the families walking on the green in front of the tower, laughing, holding each other.

No Alik wasn't hers. He couldn't be. Not ever. She repeated it over and over in her mind and tried not to give in to the ache that was climbing her throat. She wrapped her arms around herself, trying to hold the pieces of herself in, so she wouldn't go and surrender any more of herself to Alik.

Alik held Leena tightly against him and climbed up onto one of the white carousel horses, fastening them both in tightly.

He could still remember the first carousel he'd seen, in the square in Moscow. A game for children, and he'd never been a child. Not truly. So he'd never gone on it.

Leena clapped her hands and looked back up at him, her eyes, the same shade as his own, sparkled. With excitement. With trust.

Then she lifted her hand and put it on his cheek. "Da!"

And the carousel started to turn. He held tight to his daughter, held her steady on the horse. The world was turning around him, too fast to make out Jada or any other distinct shapes. Leena was all he could see.

She laughed, deep and happy as the ride turned, slapping the horses head, slapping his leg. Happiness, so pure, so unspoiled pouring out of her with ease. And the trust. That trust that Jada had spoken of.

It's yours to lose.

He didn't want to lose it. More than anything he didn't want to lose it.

Right now, at least, he had it. So he held on tight to Leena and kept his focus on her. Not on the world around them, not on the future. And he tried to grapple with the feeling of exposure, the feeling of tenderness, that was taking him over.

He didn't know himself right now. He very much doubted if he knew anything at all.

"Leena's asleep. I think we wore her out." Jada sat down next to Alik on the couch, a cup of coffee warming her palm. Alik had some sort of alcohol in his glass, and a very stoic expression on his face.

"She has a lot of energy," he said, looking down.

"She does. She liked the carousel."

"I am glad."

So, Alik wasn't going to give anything tonight. At least, nothing in terms of conversation.

"It was a good idea you had," she pushed, "taking her on it."

"Thank you."

Infuriating Russian. The man had a tendency to go Siberia cold on her whenever it suited him. "You didn't think of it last minute, though. It's what you were thinking from the beginning but you didn't want to tell me. Why?"

He looked at her, one dark brow raised. "I wasn't certain it was a good idea. I didn't know if she would like it." He said it so casually, but she had a feeling there was nothing casual in the admission. But when Alik put on his armor, that I-don't-give-a-crap facade of his, it was almost impossible to see through.

"You could have asked me."

"I didn't know if you would like it," he said.

And then she understood. That there was something personal. Something that had made him feel exposed. And he hadn't wanted her to reject it. To reject *him*.

It struck her then, that Alik felt as out of place and different in this situation as she did.

"Even if I didn't like it, I don't make all the decisions concerning Leena. You're her father—you make them too."

"I know. I understand that, but I don't know anything about children or what they're supposed to like at what age I only…"

"What?"

"Nothing."

She set her coffee mug down on the table by the sofa and put her hands in her lap, angling her body toward Alik. "You only what, Alik? Don't play stupid games with me."

"I am not playing a game," he said, standing. "I only knew that when I was a child, there was a carousel I used to walk by. After I left the orphanage. It cost money, and I would never have spent money on such a thing. I had to use what I had to buy food, or shelter if I ended up with enough. But never for something like that. Well, now I have money. Leena, by extension, has money and she can go on a carousel if she likes," he finished, his voice rough, fierce.

"Of course she can." She wasn't used to seeing Alik overcome by emotion. More and more though, it was starting to come through. More and more, he was connecting with Leena, but it was challenging him. She could see it.

And the more it came through for him, the more she felt drawn to him. And it scared her to death. Challenged her just as much as it challenged him. She didn't like the feeling she had when she was with him, and yet she craved it. So strong and compelling, so utterly frightening.

She didn't know what to call it, but she knew that Alik Vasin had a hold on her. One she couldn't shake free of. One she wanted to break away from and cling to all at the same time.

"There were no parents to care for me. To make sure I had what I needed, much less anything I wanted. I was a burden to my mother. So much so she had to give me up."

"I'm sure she wanted to keep you, Alik."

"It doesn't change anything. How she felt about it doesn't change what happened to me after. It doesn't replace what I lost." He looked down, dark eyes unfocused. "Leena deserves to have everything," he said, his voice lower now. "How will I know what to give her? I don't know what to give her."

"Just keep giving her you, Alik. She's so happy with that. Did you see her today? When you held her? She loves just being with you. She loves you."

"But what about when she realizes just what a pitiful excuse for a father I am?" he asked, his words sounding torn, broken. "When she realizes I don't know what I'm doing?"

"I don't know what I'm doing, either, Alik, I just hope that I can love her enough to cover all the mistakes I make."

"What if I can't do that, either?"

She swallowed hard, tried to speak with confidence she just didn't have. "You will."

"What if I don't?" He set his glass down hard on the mantel.

"What would you have wanted from your parents?"

"There's no point wishing for what you don't have."

"You never thought about them? Never wondered about your mother."

He shook his head once. "No."

She bit her lip, trying to keep from crying. From shouting. "But what would you have wanted? Would you have needed them to be perfect? Or would you have just needed them to be there? Just be here, Alik. Be here for her."

He paused, turning the tumbler in his hand. "I will," he said. "That I promise. I swear it."

"Then she has nothing to worry about."

Alik looked back at his glass, then back at her. His expression was raw, open, revealing the depth of his pain, his insecurity, his need. And it was so vast she was afraid that it could never, ever be filled.

Alik wasn't emotionless. Alik was hiding everything, because there was simply too much to deal with. She saw it plainly in that moment. Saw the wounds inflicted on him, over and over, during his life, and the high cost of them.

And then it was gone, replaced by the stone wall he had spent his life perfecting. "Let's go to bed," he said.

"You don't want to talk?"

"I'm done talking," he said. "I want you. Now."

"Alik…"

He stalked to the couch and bent down, bracing his hand on the back of it, his lips crashing down on hers. His kiss was rough and desperate. She was almost used to the edge of utter abandon that came with their attraction. Almost. But this was different. This wasn't about his need for her.

She didn't doubt he wanted her, after their time together she couldn't doubt that, but the need to escape that flavored his kiss wasn't about her. It was about him.

He wrapped his arm around her waist and drew her up against him, made her stand. And she clung to him, answering his need, because there was never anything else she could do with Alik.

She should resist. She shouldn't let him use her. And yet, she couldn't. She *needed* him. The moment he touched her she was lost. She had been from the moment she'd met him. She didn't know what that said about her, didn't know what it might mean. And in that moment, she honestly didn't care.

He made her want, a deep, aching want that she had yet to find satisfaction for, no matter how many times they made love. Could it even be called making love? She didn't know. She knew Alik would never call it that.

Sex isn't intimate.

Not to him.

"Alik." She said his name, pulled away and looked at his eyes.

He didn't allow it. He leaned in and kissed her neck. "Get behind the couch," he said. Hard. Demanding.

"Alik…"

"Now."

The command excited her. But everything Alik did excited her. She was experienced—she'd been married for six years—but she'd never played games like this. Though, looking at the hard glint in Alik's eye made it hard to think of it as a game. And she found that excited her even more.

She obeyed him, rounding to the back of the couch. He stood on the other side of it, watching her, his expression strangely flat. Detached.

"Hold on."

She obeyed that command too, bending at her waist and curling her fingers around the wooden frame.

"Good."

He started working his belt buckle as he rounded to the back of the couch and her heart stopped beating, climbed into her throat and made it impossible to breathe. She heard his belt slide through the loops, heard the zipper on his pants, and she tried to look back.

"Eyes ahead, princess."

And she obeyed again, because she didn't want him to stop.

He slid his hand down her back, cupped her butt, bunched the material of her dress into one hand and tugged it up. "Perfect."

He dragged her panties down her legs, and she closed her eyes, letting him touch her, tease her, heighten her arousal. And then she heard him opening a condom packet, and still she followed his orders. Still she looked ahead.

He pushed a finger deep inside of her and a sharp gasp escaped her lips.

"Ready?" he asked.

She could only nod, but it was taken as permission.

He pushed into her slowly and she dug her nails into the couch as he filled her. He went deeper at this angle and she found that she liked it. The only thing that she didn't like, was that she couldn't see him.

As he starting thrusting hard into her, she wondered if that was by design. But the thought was only a twinge of pain, swallowed quickly by the pleasure roaring through her.

Alik reached between her thighs and slid his fingers over her clitoris, bringing her release, sharp and fast, while he continued to chase his own. But even after she found hers, he didn't let up.

Tension, heat, coiled in her tightly again while he continued to work his magic on her. He slowed his rhythm, going slow so she could feel every inch of him. She bit her lip, trying to hold back the desperate whimpers that were building inside her. Trying to hold back the crash of another orgasm. She wasn't ready yet. Not yet.

One more flick of his clever fingers and he pushed her over. Her thighs were shaking, sweat beading on her brow. He kept on, pushing her higher, further.

"Alik…I can't."

"You will," he said, his voice rough, his breath hot on her neck. "With me this time."

He thrust harder, faster, his fingers moving in time with the rest of him. Impossible, she felt another wave building, bigger, frightening. It was slow, rolling, and, she feared, more than she could possibly withstand.

Alik froze, one hand gripping her hip hard, his

fingers biting into her flesh. He pulsed deep inside of her, sending her over. There was no sight, no sound, nothing but the all-consuming pleasure. She was drowning in it, in Alik.

She was still catching her breath, still trying to keep her legs from collapsing beneath her weight, when Alik moved away from her. She could hear him righting his clothes. She imagined she was allowed to look at him now. But she was afraid.

Afraid of what she might see. More afraid of what she might feel. Afraid that if she looked, there would be no more secrets at all. That he would see straight into her soul, see things no one else ever had.

He was tugging away a mask she hadn't realized she'd had. A mask kept so easily in place by her desire to please, first her parents and then her husband. She'd been happy with it. Her life had been quiet, and easy.

This wasn't quiet. It wasn't easy.

"That is more what you should expect from me," he said, his voice smug. But it was off somehow. It wasn't genuine. He was back to playing a part.

His words made her angry. Angry enough that she wasn't afraid to face him anymore. He was looking at her, his expression dispassionate, his eyes flat, his clothes righted.

"You know what, Alik, if you want to use me as your therapist, then maybe you should lie down on the couch instead of bending me over it."

"What does that mean?"

"I'm not interested in letting you use my body so you can work your issues out."

"You flatter yourself if you think sex with you is somehow connected to working out my issues."

"Do I?" she asked, her throat tightening. She wasn't going to cry. Not now. Not when he was being so spectacularly unemotional and horrible.

"I already told you, sex is sex. It's not connected to anything outside of it. It is what it is. Thank you for the orgasm."

"Stop it, Alik," she said.

"It's reality, the reality of being with me, Jada, so get used to it, or find another man."

She didn't want another man. Not any other man, not even the one she'd loved. A shocking, jolting realization.

But she didn't particularly want this one, either. Not this version of him.

"I'm going to bed," she said, turning away from him.

"No thank-you for me? I made you come three times."

She whirled around, anger coursing through her. "And? I can get my own orgasms, Alik, without having to deal with this kind of treatment after! The thing you don't understand, is that what makes sex better than your own hand is the connection you get from it. But you don't offer that and you don't accept it. So there's no point, is there?"

It wasn't true. Sex with Alik was beyond anything in her experience. But it had also forged a bond with him she didn't want. One that was tearing her apart from the inside out, stripping away every defense. The way he was acting hurt, but it wasn't why she was pulling away from him. It was because of what he made her feel.

Because of who he made her.

"I suppose not, for you. Good night."

He made no move to go. He picked his glass up from the mantel and walked over to the bar, pouring himself another drink. As if nothing had happened. Nothing that mattered. And he was dismissing her now.

"Right," she said. "Good night."

She stalked from the room, only realizing later that she'd left her underwear. If Alik didn't get them, the housekeeper would. She decided it was less of a humiliation than going back for them in Alik's presence.

So she just went up the stairs and flung her bedroom door open, and resisted the urge to slam it closed. She didn't want to give him the satisfaction of knowing how hurt she was. But then, would it even mean anything to him?

"Ah, what does this mean when you slam doors, Jada? I do not understand complex human emotion." she said to herself, imitating Alik and his accent, poorly. "It means I'm mad at you, you jackass, because you are the most insensitive and horrible human being on the planet!"

She flopped down on the bed and stared at the ceiling with gritty eyes. This was the time when she had to figure out if Alik was worth it, or if she should just abandon ship.

What do you want from him? Surely not love and marriage? Real marriage? You had that. This is not that. It never could be.

No. It never could be. Partly because Alik wasn't her first husband. And partly because she didn't think she could ever be that woman again. She was changing. But this wasn't the same kind of change she'd made in her first marriage. She wasn't changing to make Alik's life easier, to make their marriage more harmonious.

She wasn't changing to fit a mold. The change seemed endless, with no boundaries closing in. It was the kind of freedom she hadn't wanted, the kind she didn't truly understand.

She had always tried to please the people in her life, but Alik seemed to ask her to please only herself. And this woman that she was…this woman wouldn't have been happy with her life three years ago. She would have wanted more from her marriage. More passion. More honesty. Less hiding.

She was afraid of what he made her want. But she didn't want to walk away, either.

She didn't like that Alik wasn't simply in her present, that he hadn't just changed her future, but that he was changing her view of the past, as well.

CHAPTER THIRTEEN

IT HADN'T WORKED. Alik didn't like failure. He rarely failed. In fact, his only failure to date was the condom failure he'd suffered more than a year and a half ago during Leena's conception. If he'd failed otherwise, with the sorts of endeavors he'd engaged in, he would be dead.

But he had failed in putting things back into place inside himself. He had failed in his attempt to feel normal again after the carousel ride with Leena.

He had failed in holding Jada at a reasonable distance. He had failed in putting her back there. He had tried.

He'd thought if he couldn't see her face. If he just took it back to sex at its most basic, then he would stop aching inside. That it would give him the high, the euphoria that sex had always given him.

But sex with Jada had a cost. And each time it seemed higher.

If only the price could be paid in money. He had

that. This was asking for pieces of him, demanding he lower his guard to pay, and he really didn't like that. He had emotions. He knew it now. But he'd built up a wall around them so thick, so high, that not even he had been able to pull it down at his own whim.

He'd given all the credit to Leena before. But Jada was the one with the wrecking ball. She was taking down his defenses, and everything was spilling out now. Years of need, of unmet emotional longing, bleeding endlessly from him.

He found he couldn't even scowl about it, because he was, at that moment, sitting on the floor in Leena's room, watching his daughter toddle around in a circle. She was wearing a short, pink dress that showed off chubby legs, the skirt flaring out in the back, thanks to her diaper.

"Fashion forward," he said to her, as she wobbled and her legs folded, dropping her straight on her bottom. "And practical for you, I imagine it cushioned you some."

She gurgled and let out a long string of jabber that she seemed to think were words, because when she was done, she looked at him expectantly.

"I don't know what you said."

She responded with more jabber and flapping

hands. In spite of his foul mood, he felt a smile curve his lips. Jada was right about one thing, babies were very cute. Although, he didn't think babies in general were all that cute. But Leena was. Leena was the most beautiful thing he had ever seen. So perfect and tiny.

He shifted and lay down on his stomach, propping himself up on his elbow and taking her hand in his. He counted her fingers. Five of them. Then he took her other hand and counted the fingers there too before moving on to her toes.

"Ten and ten," he said. "Had to check."

"That was the first thing I did when I held her at the hospital."

He looked over his shoulder and straightened into a sitting position. "Is it?"

"Yes." Jada walked into the room and he wondered how long she'd been standing there. He didn't like her being witness to all this stuff. Mainly because he didn't want anyone to witness it. These feelings for Leena, the feelings he kept having in general, were like new skin growing over wounds. Tender. Raw.

"I wanted to make sure."

"Well, yeah. You have to do it."

"I didn't get to hold her at the hospital," he said,

suddenly choked by regret. "I wish I would have known about her. And I hope if I had I would have cared."

"Are you honestly afraid you wouldn't have?"

"Seeing Sayid with his family…that started changing my thoughts on babies. But…a year ago? I'm not certain what I would have done."

"You would have done the right thing, Alik. Because it's what you do."

"No, Jada, it's not." He pushed up into standing and Leena shrieked, holding her arms up and looking at him plaintively. He couldn't deny her. He bent and picked her up and she giggled, triumphant. "I've spent my life doing what was best for me and to hell with everyone else."

"What changed?"

"I don't know. Maybe me. We can only hope."

Except last night he'd done it with Jada. Done what pleased himself. Had looked out only for his own well-being. Although, it hadn't gone as planned. There had been none of the detachment he'd bragged about to her in the beginning.

"Do you want to change, Alik?"

"If it's possible."

"You hurt me last night," she said.

Her words hit him like a slap to the face. "Where? What did I do?"

"Not physically," she said, her cheeks coloring. "Physically it all felt good. But the way you treated me after… Alik, I understand that you don't want love and all of that—that's fine. But I don't want you to try and prove the point that you feel nothing every time you're with me."

"Do you want love, Jada?"

She shook her head slowly. "Not from you."

He didn't know why, but the admission stabbed at him. "Then what is it you want from me?"

"Respect. Being treated like more than a whore."

"I don't treat you like that."

"You do. You did last night. Like a woman who was there just to satisfy you."

"I gave you pleasure," he said, "more than I did the night that…"

"You know what? I preferred the night you came first," she said, the color in her cheeks deepening.

"How?"

"Last night was balm for your ego, Alik. You can't pretend otherwise. So you proved you were a stud and you…" Her eyes drifted to Leena. "I know she doesn't know what we're talking about but I can't help thinking that this could be a scarring early life experience for her."

Alik set his daughter down in her crib and put a shape sorter in front of her, and even though she shot him an indignant look, she didn't scream. "Outside."

He and Jada walked out of the nursery and he closed the door behind them. "You may finish telling me why I left you sexually unsatisfied now," he said dryly.

"You were proving something about yourself," she said. "You weren't giving to me. That other time? You just lost control. And I think I liked that better. It was honest, at least. I'm tired of... I'm tired of not having honesty."

"When have I not given you honesty?"

"You did at first, but now...now you're protecting yourself and I've had that relationship, Alik. Where everyone is hiding what they want so they don't hurt anyone, so they don't hurt themselves."

"I thought you didn't want love."

"I don't."

"Then why bother to make comparisons?"

"You're right. I shouldn't. But I would rather have fast, than pleasure brought from your calculated control."

"That makes no sense, Jada. Sex is about pleasure."

"That's not all it's about. Didn't you hear what I said to you last night?"

Yes. He'd heard it. That she would have been better off alone than with him when it came to getting pleasure. He hadn't liked it at all. The rejection had cut through his compromised defenses with stunning accuracy.

"Hard to miss."

"Sex is about intimacy with someone. About connection. It's not about an adrenaline rush, or feeling good for a few minutes. Until you realize that you're missing out on a huge piece of what sex is. You're missing out on making love."

"And you're an expert?"

"Alik, I've had the best sex with you. No question. In terms of pleasure, in terms of excitement… I didn't have any clue it could be so good. But I'm lonely after. And I'm cold. And I've had quite enough of that."

He didn't like hearing that. That he hurt her. That he was spreading the chill inside of his soul to her. She was so warm, so beautiful and full of light. Thinking he might be damaging that…the pain of it stabbed right through the walls he kept around his heart.

"I am sorry for that," he said. "It wasn't my intention to hurt you."

He'd been too busy trying to protect himself to worry about what pushing Jada away might do to her, because until he'd listened to her talk just now, he hadn't truly understood how sex could be connected to emotion. To the way you felt about yourself.

That wasn't entirely true. He'd been on a journey to understanding it since the first time he'd touched her. Because when they were done, the feel of her lingered. Her smell haunted him, feminine and exotic, jasmine and spice and pure enticement.

He had never been able simply to have her and put her out of his mind. He'd never been able to look at her and then put her out of his mind. Like her spice lingered on his skin, Jada always lingered in his thoughts.

"I know, Alik. You never intend to hurt anyone. You just don't always understand how other people…feel."

He didn't. Because he didn't feel in the same way other people did. And he hated that in himself now. Hated it because it had caused Jada pain. Because it might cause Leena pain later.

"I always thought if I smiled enough," he said,

"then I would start to feel happy. If I did enough things that made me feel good, it might turn into something more. It doesn't work that way. It never made me feel a damn thing. But Leena does. You do."

"Me?" she asked, her cheeks paled.

"Yes. I am sorry I hurt you. Knowing that I did… it hurts me."

"Empathy."

He nodded slowly. "New for me. I am pleased to have found it. I owe you, for the way I treated you last night."

She shook her head, her dark ponytail swinging in time with the movement. "No, you don't, Alik. That's not how it works. It's not a trade system. Just don't do it again."

"I want to take you out," he said. He did. He wanted to make her smile. Wanted to be in public with her at his side, wanted to show everyone that she was his. It was a strange desire, new. So many new feelings and needs in the past few weeks. He was starting to feel like a different man. Finally. After so many years of trying.

"What about Leena?"

"Marie is here."

"I know, but I don't like giving her all the responsibility." Jada had a hard time giving up control to the au pair, but Alik, selfishly, liked that it ensured she had more free time in the evenings with him.

"One night out is hardly giving her all the responsibility. Please, come with me."

"All right, but I have to change. I'm not going out in my sweats."

"Wear something red."

"I haven't been to a club in...maybe ever," Jada said, eyeing the crowded room. People were seated at bistro tables that circled the dance floor, all of it packed in tight. The concept of personal space a total loss.

It wasn't like a flashing lights techno club or anything, for which she was grateful. It was dark and smoky, live jazz music provided by a band on stage.

"You've never been to a club?"

"I got married very young and got busy with being a homemaker. We went out, but not dancing. And certainly not anywhere like this."

"Didn't you ever want to?"

"We just...we didn't."

He frowned. "And now, are you here because of

me only? Because it is something we do? Or do you want to be here?"

"I want to be here, but it's not…it's not like he was holding me back. At least, I didn't think so. I liked what we had. Yes, the baby thing caused some problems but I know we would have worked it out."

"But tonight you want to dance?"

"Yes. Tonight I want to dance."

Alik tightened his hold on her and turned her to face him, his eyes skimming over her body. She had followed his order and put on a short, red dress that hugged her figure a bit more lovingly than she normally cared for. Or maybe that wasn't true anymore.

This was a dress she'd bought last week, and it had seemed perfect. And she'd had Alik in mind when she'd bought it. He was even changing her taste in clothes.

"The last time I danced was at my first wedding," she said.

"Too long, Jada."

He released his hold on her, then laced his fingers through hers, leading her into the center of the packed dance floor. The crush of bodies around them wrapped them in an intimate cocoon and when Alik pulled her against his arms, she melted into him.

They danced slowly, her head tucked against his chest. It was so simple, so romantic.

"This doesn't seem like the kind of club a billionaire would frequent," she said, trying to dispel some of the misty haze that had descended around them.

"Maybe it isn't, but it's exactly the kind of place I used to go to when I came to Paris for the first time. I thought it would be nice to…show you. To share with you."

That made her heart tighten. "Thank you."

The music stopped for a moment, then the bassist started plucking strings, fast and hard, setting up a rhythm that didn't support the gentle sway she and Alik had been moving in. A smile curved Alik's lips and he dropped his hands from around her waist, took her hands in his.

She wasn't experienced at dancing, but Alik was easy to follow. He twirled her and drew her into his body before releasing her again. She laughed, a light, fizzing sensation filling her chest, her head.

The music kept going and she kicked her shoes off at some point, throwing them under one of the bistro tables. She and Alik danced until her brow was damp with sweat, until her voice was hoarse from singing and laughing.

"Last song," Alik said, in response to the announcement from the lead singer. "Want to dance to it?"

"I'm going to fall over, Alik. You've exhausted me," she said, wandering back to the table and bracing her hand on the surface, tugging her shoes out from beneath it and putting them back on. "That was…fun." The most fun she could remember having in years. "Thank you. I didn't know I would like dancing so much." It was on the tip of her tongue to say they should go again. That she wanted to make it a regular thing. But there was no point to that. None at all.

"I didn't, either," he said. He took her hand and led her out of the club, back into the crisp night air. It felt cool and dry on her skin after the moist heat of the dance floor. "I didn't know a lot of things about life until you, Jada," he said, pulling her close, kissing her lips. It was tender, sweet. Frightening.

"I want you to teach me," he said, his voice rough.

"Teach you what?" she asked.

People were leaving clubs all along the street,

weaving around where she and Alik were standing. But she didn't want to move, didn't want to break the spell of the moment.

"Teach me what it means to make love."

No. Her heart screamed in denial. The request, so simple, was scarier than anything else she'd faced with him. And now she wondered if she should have simply been content with their encounter on the couch. If she should never have told him she needed more. Because this was too much. Too close to her deepest fear.

She'd been with him so many times, and yet, this was the time she feared might break her. Because he wasn't asking for her body. He was asking for her soul. Asking her to go deeper than she felt she could.

The further she went with Alik, the more distant her past became. The less her image of the past appealed, because the woman she was turning into wouldn't fit into it.

She was terrified of losing it, of dishonoring it. Of what it would mean if she took another step away from it, another step toward becoming this person who seemed almost entirely different than the one she'd been with her husband.

All she had were her memories, and the way she saw those was changing, too.

She was trembling inside, but as she looked up into Alik's eyes, she knew she could deny him nothing. "Yes. I'll teach you, Alik."

He had the strongest desire to get drunk. To ask Jada for a reprieve when they got back to his town house so that he could stop by the bar and down a few shots.

But when he stopped and looked at Jada in the bright light of the entryway, in her short red dress that revealed her tanned, toned legs, he was grateful for his sobriety.

Still, when she approached him, he shook like an adolescent. He couldn't recall ever feeling nervous before sex. Not even his first time. He'd been too filled with the kind of bravado a teenage boy who'd spent his life on the streets needed in order to survive.

But he felt on the verge of coming undone now. Yet if he did anything to dull the experience, he knew he would miss something. Because with Jada, he always wanted to feel it all. Hot, rough, perfect. And every time she left him hungrier for more.

She was already beneath his skin in a way no

other woman had ever been. Was there any point in fighting? Not tonight. Not now. Now he was going to embrace it, because this was the kind of feeling he'd been chasing all of his life.

There was no drug, no alcohol, no beautiful woman, who had ever brought him this close to the edge of ecstasy. Just looking at Jada put him there. And it wasn't just the promise of physical pleasure. It was all-encompassing heat. Like standing in front of a fire, warming every piece of him, burning inside and out.

He had tried to create something like this for most of his life. Had tried to heat the frozen spaces, tried to bring to life parts of him that were dead.

Here he was now, and he was afraid. Afraid he couldn't handle it. Afraid she would be displeased with him. When all of his protection burned away, and left only Alik, would she still want him?

He didn't have time to dwell on that. He couldn't. Because she was walking toward him now, and her eyes were focused on his. As though she saw into him. As though she saw everything. It was impossible, of course. Because if she could truly see into him, if she could see all he had been, if she could truly understand the pain, the damage that was beneath the stone walls around his heart, she would turn away.

But she didn't. She kept walking to him.

"As exciting as I found the couch, I thought we might make use of the bed tonight."

"You're in charge tonight," he said. "This is all you."

"No, Alik, this is us." She held her hand out and he took it, her soft, delicate fingers curling around his, her thumb skimming a rough patch of skin on his wrist. Her fingers were unsteady and he saw that her eyes were glistening. He couldn't figure out why. And he cursed his inability to simply understand her emotion. "This whole night is about us. That's the first difference between sex and making love. It's not my pleasure. It's not your pleasure. It's ours."

He nodded slowly, his heart thundering, low and steady. She led him from the room and up the stairs and he felt a tremor go up his spine. He laughed.

"What?" she asked, turning to him, the light from the top of the stairs backlighting her, hiding her expression.

"I have faced down enemy gunfire and not felt any fear. There is little fear in death to me. And this, connecting with another person? That's frightening."

"I trust you're brave enough to withstand a night of making love with me." She leaned in and kissed him, her lips soft, perfection.

And he wasn't so sure. It took everything in him not to pick her up and carry her in the room for a bit of hard and fast. That was easy. That was all physical release. This, this slow walk was forcing him to let the pressure build.

He wanted to hide behind what he knew. Wanted to take charge. But he was too fascinated, and he was far too self-destructive to turn away from something that had this much power to wound.

A sobering and very true realization about himself. Hadn't he spent all of his life acting like whether he lived or died didn't matter? Hadn't he spent his life daring whoever was in charge of the universe to simply finish the job? Rather than having him exist, a physical, intact body that was empty inside?

This might be the thing that set him free, that took all the walls down, once and for all. Or it would be the thing that secured his place in hell.

He only hoped he didn't bring Jada down with him.

They went into his room this time. They'd never been together in his room. Because it put Jada in control of what happened afterward. Whether she left. Whether she stayed.

"Take your clothes off," she said.

He obeyed, and she did the same. Then when they were both naked, they lay down on the bed. She wrapped her arms around him and held him against her, burying her face in his neck, inhaling deeply.

She sighed. It was a sweet sound. One of contentment, of happiness. It made emotion swell in his chest, emotion he wanted to push down. If he just rolled her onto her back, he could take her, bring her to the height of pleasure and make her forget about this.

But he wanted to keep the torture going. Wanted to wallow in this newfound form of punishment. A vision of what could be. If only. If only he wasn't broken beyond repair.

She leaned in and kissed him. Slow and deep, erotic torment for his body and soul. She was attuned to him, to every tensing of his muscles, to every sound of pleasure. Her kiss was for him. Just for him. And he wanted to give her pleasure like it in return. Not just pleasure derived from his knowledge about sex and his experience with it, but knowledge from his experiences with Jada.

And so he did. He tore his mouth from hers, then dropped a teasing kiss back on her mouth, took her lower lip between his teeth and bit her gently, because he knew she liked it.

He was rewarded with a low hum and a sweet smile, and it only made his chest feel fuller. Made his whole body feel like it was trying to hold something far too big for one man to carry.

But too wonderful to pass off to anyone else. Jada was his. This was his.

He lowered his head, pressed a kiss to the valley between her breasts. "You are the most beautifully formed woman I have ever seen," he said.

He cupped her, traced the outline of her nipple with the tip of his tongue before sucking it deep into his mouth. She arched into him, her fingers laced in his hair. And he smiled against her skin. She always did that. Always held on to him as though he was anchoring her to earth.

He loved it.

Her skin was soft beneath his hands, and he traced her curves with his fingertips, memorizing every inch of her. There had never been another woman like her. At the moment, he couldn't even remember another woman. They were inconsequential. Everything was.

The violence, the pain, it all fell away beneath Jada's hands. Her touch burned away the memory of everything else. Her voice, soft, sweet, whispering things in his ear, promises of pleasure, words of encouragement, drowned out the visions of violence, the hard, angry, ugly words he'd been exposed to from the time he was a boy.

And when he slid inside of her, it was like the world fell away. And there was nothing but the two of them. And they didn't even seem like two people anymore.

She wrapped her legs around his waist, moving in time with him, until he could no longer tell who was in control, could no longer tell where he ended and she began.

He felt her tense beneath him, felt her internal muscles tighten around him, and he let go. Let his release wash over him in a wave, drowning out sound and light, pouring through him, into every part of him.

He thought his heart would burst through his chest, thought the walls would cave in around him. But when he came back to himself, everything was the same.

And nothing was. He felt changed. Totally and completely.

Jada wrapped her arms around him, and he adjusted himself, pulling her against him. She rested her head on his chest, her hand over his heart.

And for the first time in his life, Alik wasn't in a hurry to leave the woman by his side. He wasn't on to the next time or place in his mind. On to the next lover. Jada filled his senses, and he was happy to leave it that way. Replete. Satisfied.

"The anchor doesn't mean nothing," he said, not sure why he felt compelled to share. Except it seemed right. After experiencing intimacy with Jada it seemed right to try and deepen it.

"The anchor?" she said, her voice sleepy.

He lifted his arm and showed her the tattoo. "They told me my father was in the navy. At the orphanage. At least, I think that's what my mother told them. I have no idea if it's true. But I thought… I thought it might make me feel closer to him. Sailors have tattoos like this and I thought we might share a trait. I was seventeen, on the run, making my way through Asia and I thought it might make me feel connected with someone. With something. It was stupid. It didn't work, either. I like the tattoo, though."

"I like your tattoos," she said, tracing the line on the anchor with her fingertip. "They keep the past close to you. Permanent reminders of a place you used to be."

Jada looked up at him, the sadness in her eyes stealing his breath. And he wondered who had put it there. If it was past memories, or if it was his fault somehow.

"Memories are good," he said. "But there is no time in my past I would choose to return to."

He watched her face closely, watched pain flash across her face. He reached out to cup her cheek and she turned away from him. Then she sat up, clutching the blanket to her chest. "I should go back to bed. I need to be by Leena's room."

"You should be able to hear if…"

"But I might not be able to," she said. She got out of bed and picked her clothes up off the floor, dressing quickly.

Was this how she felt every night when he left her? Bare? Exposed? Rejected? Because he felt every bit of that and more.

"Don't go."

"It's just…better. I'll see you in the morning."

She turned around and left, shutting the door behind her. Tonight, Alik had had his first taste of true intimacy. And his first taste of what it was to have intimacy rejected.

The latter made him feel that the former was unbelievably overrated.

There was no way he was sleeping tonight. He got up and put on his sweats and running shoes. He had to think. And in order to do that, he needed to run. And he wouldn't stop until he came up with an answer to the burning hunger in his chest.

CHAPTER FOURTEEN

"Good morning, Alik."

"Good morning," he said, sitting down at the breakfast table. Leena was in her usual position and Jada was in hers.

Funny how they all had usual positions now. Jada wanted to scream and run from it. Why hadn't she realized just how much making love with Alik would cost her? She'd thought she could do it. She'd thought she was strong enough. And now she was coming apart inside. Over crepes and coffee. Which was about the stupidest thing ever.

"Breakfast is really, really good this morning," she said, her words shaky as she spooned a bite of banana, wrapped in crepe and cream, into Leena's mouth.

"It looks like it." Alik sat down across from her, his expression sober, and his eyes far too perceptive. "Finish eating because I want to talk to you."

"I'm taking Leena out for a walk so maybe after…"

"I have called Marie and she will be by to walk Leena. You're going to talk to me."

She nodded slowly. "I'll just finish up my coffee."

"Or bring it into the sitting room with me."

Just then, the lovely, dark-haired woman who took care of Leena walked onto the patio. *"Bonjour."*

"Marie, can you finish giving Leena her breakfast?"

"Of course!" she answered far too brightly. So brightly it gave Jada a headache. And stole her excuse for avoiding Alik.

Jada stood grudgingly and Alik did, too, but not before he dropped a kiss on Leena's head. The sight made Jada's heart crack further. He loved Leena. She saw it whenever he looked at her, and now…he could even show it.

It was all she'd needed. For Leena and for him. And it made what she had to do now, what she had to do for her, easier.

Not easier, nothing would make it easier, but it made it less risky. She'd taught Alik to love and he didn't need her anymore. Not as a lover.

And she couldn't afford to play with fire anymore.

"Why are you running from me, Jada?" he asked when they were alone.

"I'm not. But now that you mention it, there is something going on. Something I've been thinking about since last night."

"What?"

"We always said this…this thing between us would end, and I think it needs to end now."

Alik looked like she'd slapped him. "What?"

"It's going to end, Alik, and I want to do it now. While we like each other. While we respect each other and…you're such a good father. You're doing amazing with Leena and…"

"Bull."

"What?"

"You're lying. You don't want to end things while we like each other. I don't believe you." He was right. She was lying. But she had to do it. Everything she'd been, everything that had mattered, was starting to get fuzzy in her mind as Alik grew clearer, sharper. She didn't understand her feelings. She didn't understand herself.

"We talked about this. It was always going to end, and I think we need to do it while everything is healthy between us."

"What is healthy about two people who can't

keep their hands off each other, Jada? Tell me. What is healthy about that? I am not an expert on healthy human behavior so I can't comment."

"It's passing," she said.

"Is it?" he bit out.

"It is for me," she said, the lie stabbing at her deep.

"Don't end things."

"Why?"

Alik looked down, then at her, his gray eyes blazing with intensity. "I have fallen in love with you."

It was the admission she'd longed for most. The one she'd feared the most. The one she absolutely couldn't answer. "No, Alik, you haven't."

"Are you going to tell me now what I feel, Jada? Because you are an expert on emotion and I know nothing?"

She almost laughed. She'd never felt less expert in her life. She felt so confused, so crippled by pain and uncertainty. But she had to do this. "That's not it, it's just…this has been a very different and challenging time for you and I think you might be…"

"No. Jada, if you don't want this then say it, but don't you dare question what I feel. I damn well love you and I will not have you force me to deny it."

"I don't want you to love me."

"I don't care," he said, advancing on her, grabbing her hands and tugging her against his chest. "I don't care what you want. I love you. I have never loved anything in all my life until I saw that child in the courthouse. It burned me, Jada. It burned my heart to see her. My flesh and blood, the only flesh and blood I have. And then there was you. So bright and fiery, challenging me, tempting me." He dipped his head, his lips a whisper from hers. "You let me inside you…doesn't that count for anything?"

She felt light-headed, pain slicing through her like a knife's blade. But it was nothing compared to the fear. Nothing compared to the terror she felt at the idea of losing him. The thought of caring enough, of giving enough of herself to him that if he were ever gone from her she would never be able to put herself back together.

She pulled away from him, swaying on her feet. "You don't understand, Alik. I've had love," she said. "And this isn't it. This isn't…this isn't what it feels like. This isn't me."

"Of course it's not the same—I'm not the same

man he was. You're not the same woman you were. You've walked through hell. Did you honestly think you would come out the other side needing the same things you needed before you went in?"

"Of course I'm not the same! There's no way I could be. But what you're asking? It's impossible. You want me to just forget him, to…"

"I never said I wanted you to forget him."

"What other option is there? I'm getting further and further away from him and I can't even…I can't even capture the way that I used to feel anymore. I have been…drowning in this grief and pain for so long, and before that I had a life. I had a life and dreams enough for the future, and if I just keep…moving away from it, then what did it mean? It's like I'm making it so it doesn't even matter."

"Why can't it matter, too? Why can't you just let it go and…"

"How would you even know what I can and can't let go of, Alik? What any person could? You've clung to your pain, shielded it, all your life. You've spent all these years running from your feelings, from your pain, so don't you dare tell me what I should let go of!"

He advanced on her, his lip curled into a snarl.

"You're right—I've spent enough time running, Jada, so I know what that looks like. But you aren't even running. You're just standing in the same spot, glued to it because you're afraid to move on. I know your path changed, I know it's rough and scary and I know it hurts, but you still have to walk on it, dammit. You were the one that told me life moves on. But you aren't moving, Jada. You're standing still."

"So I should just go on like he didn't matter? Like everything is fine?"

"You didn't die three years ago. He did," Alik said, his voice hard. Angry.

"Stop. Just stop."

"No. You listen. You are alive, Jada Patel, but you choose to bury yourself. To try to live unchanging and unmoving. There is life here. There could be life with me. But you won't take it."

Her eyes glistened, with tears. With anger. "Just because I don't want you doesn't mean I don't want to live," she said. "I did change. I got Leena, didn't I?"

"You didn't change—you simply didn't have anyone standing in the way of what you always wanted. Because he did stand in your way, Jada, whether you want to admit it or not. He stood in the way of Leena. Of who you are."

"He didn't, Alik. He was a good man, he—"

"Better than me?"

"Yes." He jerked back, as though he'd been slapped. But still she kept going. "I want a simple, normal life that doesn't hurt all the time. I want to raise my daughter, with you because you're her father and it's right, but I don't want to be your wife."

"You are in luck, then," he said slowly, taking an envelope off the desk. "The adoption is finalized. You don't have to be my wife."

She blinked slowly. "I don't?"

"No."

"Oh."

"You listen to me," he said. "I will divorce you. I will give you what you ask for. I will put you in a house of your choosing. Here, in Attar, in New York, back in Oregon. I don't care. But before I do that, I am going to say it one more time and when you reject it, you be sure that you don't want it because I will never say it again…do you understand me? Reject me again and I withdraw it."

She closed her eyes, a tear sliding down her cheek. And she nodded, biting her lip, trying to hold the pain at bay.

"I love you."

She shook her head, a sob escaping her lips, more tears falling. "No." It was all she could say.

"Then that is the last time I will torture you with the words. Now get out."

"Alik…"

"Out."

Alik watched Jada walk out of the room, and he felt his chest tear in two. It was like everything in him had come to life, new and raw and bleeding. He felt it all now. The loss, so intense, crippling, and with it, the love that beat behind it. Too strong to be wiped out, no matter how cruel the rejection.

This was why he had left himself numb for so long.

Because his life would have been nothing but an endless hell of pain if he hadn't learned to numb it. But if he had spent his life feeling, then perhaps this moment wouldn't be quite so devastating. Perhaps he could have built up a security system against it. As it was, there was nothing to prepare him for it. For how it felt to tell a woman he loved her. To have her throw it back at him.

He wanted to hurt her, as he was hurting. He wanted to take Leena from her. Just for one, small, ugly moment, he wanted it. And then he imagined the pain it would put her through and his own doubled.

Love was hell. To want to make her feel his pain, to know that if he did it would hurt him even more.

No wonder he had guarded himself against this. He had been smart.

He wished he could close himself up again. Wished he could go back to life before Jada. Wished he could unlearn intimacy. Wished he had never made love with her.

But if he wished it all away, if he turned back to the man he was, then he would lose his love for Leena, too. And Leena was worth the pain. She was worth any pain.

So strange. He had lived his life for so long, and he had had nothing to live for. So he had flirted with death. With danger. Now he had something that was truly worth dying for. He would lay down his life for Leena without hesitation, but for her sake, for the love of her, he wanted to live now more than he ever had.

He also wanted to cut his heart out of his chest.

It was too damned early in the day to drink. And he had no way to numb his pain. So instead he walked out of the sitting room and back to the patio. Marie was still there talking to Leena.

"Let me take her," he said.

He picked her up and smelled her hair, and a strange feeling of calm cut through the pain. He had Leena. No matter what, he had Leena.

He didn't need Jada. He only needed his daughter. And he wouldn't hurt his daughter by taking her from his wife. The woman who would be his ex-wife soon enough.

After giving Leena back to Marie, he walked outside into the chilly Parisian morning and did his best to ignore the word. Ex-wife. It kept repeating itself in his mind. Over and over again, in time with his footsteps.

He gritted his teeth. It didn't matter. She didn't matter. He had made a vow. He would not tell her he loved her again. He would not even think it. Jada had missed her chance with him. She could have her freedom. She could have her safety.

She could cling to the memory of a husband who could no longer hold her.

He would not look back. He would not offer his love again.

He'd sent Jada and Leena back to Attar, while he'd taken a different plane, had gone back to Brussels to check on his earlier deal. The one that had been interrupted by the discovery of his child. And the acquisition of his new wife.

Now he was walking downtown, the streets cold and wet, the clubs inviting. In there was every tool he needed to forget. Women. Alcohol. Especially women.

He jerked open the door to one of the clubs. The music, cigarette smoke and thick smell of sweat and booze hit him hard. It was all so familiar. So much more familiar than this feeling of raw vulnerability in his chest.

Here, there was no pain. No need to be honest. Here, there was oblivion. Shallow and perfect. The strobe lights were blinding, the bass deafening. A hostile takeover of the senses. Everything he could have asked for.

He went to the bar and ordered a drink, then surveyed his surroundings. Until he spotted her. Blonde, tall and bombshell curvy. All the things Jada wasn't.

She was leaning against the other end of the bar, a drink in her hand. She lifted a toothpick from it and put it in her mouth, sucking the cherry from the end. Subtle she was not. Good. He didn't want subtle.

He wanted easy.

He put his glass to his lips and made eye contact with her. And on cue, she worked her way down the bar toward him, her hips swaying. He felt no desire for her. But this wasn't about her.

"Buy me another drink?" she shouted over the music.

He nodded and signaled to the bartender.

He knew the steps to this dance. Everything about it was familiar. Except for the sick feeling in his stomach. Except for the total absence of adrenaline. Of the thrill.

The woman approached him, put her hand over his, tilted her head to the side. She talked. She played with her hair. She licked her lips.

His vision blurred. Until he saw Jada. In a white dress, walking down the aisle toward him like she was going to the gallows.

And then he heard their vows. Over and over again.

Promises of togetherness until death. Of faithfulness.

And Sayid's words, echoing in his head.

You think what happened here today, the words you spoke, you think those won't matter?

It mattered. Regardless of what he wanted to believe. It mattered.

She mattered. And the simple act of her not returning his love didn't erase it.

"I have to go." He put his drink down on the bar and turned away from the woman, walked back toward the door.

Someone ran into him, laughed, a strange-sounding laugh. Drunken. Not genuine.

No wonder he had never found anything lasting here. No wonder this had never brought him satisfaction. There was nothing real in this. Nothing of substance.

Jada and Leena were the real thing.

They were all that mattered. And if he had to put himself through the pain of her rejection a thousand times, he would do it.

Because before Jada, he had been a prisoner in himself. And now, pain and all, he was free.

Alik had been gone for days, leaving Leena and Jada alone in Attar.

Jada couldn't complain. She badly needed the space. Needed to get her head on straight. Find herself again, whoever that was.

Although the idea that space would somehow ease her pain was terribly flawed. She knew that. Space, separation, caused so much pain.

Leena had fallen asleep already, which was nice in some ways. Not in others. Because without her daughter to entertain, all Jada had were her thoughts. And her thoughts were a sad, bitter place at the moment.

Bitter at herself, mostly. And at Alik for demanding so much of her.

Jada sighed and rested her arms on the railing, looking out over the ocean. She missed Alik. She missed his touch. His kiss. His laugh. She missed how she felt happy around him.

You're not the same woman you were.

She couldn't get his words out of her mind. That was what scared her. That she'd changed so much. That all her memories were fading into a vague, colorless past. Happy, but no longer so poignant. No longer something she felt desperate to recapture. No longer something she idolized as utter perfection, but something she now saw as flawed. Real.

She was standing on the edge of a cliff, and she wasn't sure whether or not she should jump. She was afraid that by embracing her new self with Alik, she would lose who she'd been with Sunil.

But Sunil was gone. And there was no way to know how things would have played out if he was still here. No way to know how she would have changed, or not changed.

The simple truth was, the woman who was here and now, wanted Alik, and no other man. The woman she was now wouldn't go back, because this life, her life, was everything she hadn't known she'd wanted. And she wanted Alik, so much. So incredibly much. His touch, his laugh, him.

She waited for the guilt that admission should bring, but there was none. Just a sort of sweet ache in her heart.

She closed her eyes and lifted her face to the sky, the ocean breeze skimming over her skin like a caress. That made her think of Alik, too. When she thought of the word *husband,* it was his face she saw. When she thought of love…

She couldn't go forward while she had one foot in the past. She realized that now. She also realized that she'd been doing it by design. That she'd been doing it to keep herself safe.

But Alik, stupid Alik, sexy, wonderful Alik, wouldn't let her stay safe.

He had pulled her open, exposed her, made her care and laugh and love. Made her hunger for life, for the next chapter instead of the ones at the beginning of the book.

She had been terrified of shedding her old self. That her new skin seemed to fit so much better. Because she hadn't been sure how to reconcile it all. She had been happy with Sunil. But…but with Alik there was the promise of something true. Something complete. And it had all been too much for her to handle.

And now she'd ruined everything. Alik would never offer his love to her again. His face when he'd said that…it had been so cold. So horribly cold.

"How dare you?"

She turned and saw Alik, walking toward her. He was wearing the remnants of a suit, no tie, his shirt rumpled and the sleeves pushed up to his elbows.

"How dare I what?"

"How dare you…storm into my life."

"You were the one who stormed into mine," she said.

"Then why am I the one left devastated?"

She flinched, the haunted look in his eyes almost too painful for her to witness.

He took her arm and pulled her to him, his expression fierce. "You stripped me of all of my protection. Of everything that was holding me together. And then you took yourself from me too."

"How dare I?" she asked. "How dare you! I feel like…I don't even know who I am anymore. No, that's not it. I feel like I found myself for the first time and I have nothing to hide behind. I have no excuse now, not to be this person, not to…not to grab what I want and I'm afraid of what I want, Alik. Of how badly I want it."

"And what is it you want?"

"You," she breathed. "No matter what…I…all I want is you. I've made some bad choices lately."

"You have?" he asked, his expression frozen.

She nodded. "Alik, I was so stupid. I was so focused on protecting things that have already passed that I missed something I could have had now. I was too…I was too afraid of the person I was becoming and it made me want to cling to the past even more."

"Emotion," he said slowly, "is a very strange thing. As I am learning. I tried to feel for most of my life, and I failed. I tried to create deep feelings from shallow things but that doesn't work. You can't protect yourself and embrace love."

"Sometimes you can't stop it, either, even

though you want to. I wanted to stop it, Alik, but I couldn't."

He laughed. "You wanted to stop what, princess?" The tenderness in his voice made her want to cry. Then she realized she was already crying.

She wiped a tear from her cheek. "Alik, I tried so hard to fix you because it was easier than looking at myself and seeing what a mess I still was. I was so afraid that wanting different things now, becoming a different person now, would make my marriage obsolete. That it would dishonor my husband's memory. More than that even…that I just wouldn't be able to hide anything of myself. You distracted me, made me start to forget."

"My sex appeal, I think."

"You *would* think that, and I won't lie, it was that in the beginning."

"And now?"

"I am the most self-righteous, ridiculous, un-self-aware person on the planet."

"Are you?"

"I must be. I had myself convinced that my past was perfection."

"And I know that I'm not perfection."

Her heart seized. "Alik…no…let me finish. I thought moving on from my past would somehow be disloyal or that it would…that it would erase it. That wanting something different now might mean that what I had then was somehow less. Alik, you made me want again. You made me dream. You took me dancing. You made me happy. You showed me that I wanted things I hadn't even known I wanted. And with all of that…I don't need my memories anymore. And those memories meant so much. They're warm and sweet, calm. They're what my idea of love was."

"We are not sweet and calm, are we?"

"No. We aren't. You challenge me. You arouse me like no other man ever has. I've spent my life doing things exactly how I should, and no one has ever made me want to deviate from that path. But you…you had me up against a wall in an opera house! You make me lose my control. You make me dizzy. And this isn't anything I've ever felt before, anything I ever wanted before. And I didn't understand how this could be me. I didn't understand how this thing between you and me could be love."

He put his hand on her cheek, his eyes filled with sadness so deep it made her heart squeeze. "For you, maybe it isn't."

She shook her head. "No. You were right. It's

different because you're different. Because I'm different. Because I need to be different. I realized it then, Alik. And that was when I ran. When you said you loved me, I had to face the fact that I loved you, too, and…"

"You love me?"

She nodded, the words sticking in her throat.

"Then why did you…why did you walk away from me?"

"I was running. You should know all about that."

He slid his thumbs over her cheeks, wiping her tears away. "Will you stop running from me? Will you stop running from us? I have. I tried to go back, Jada. I'm not proud of it. I tried to go to a club, to pick up a woman. I found I didn't even want to. I couldn't. I am too changed by what has passed between us."

She nodded. "I am, too. I don't want to go back, either, and that's what scared me, Alik. That I've moved on. Finally. Really."

He took her hands in his, pinned them to his chest. "I have broken down every wall inside of myself so that there could be nothing between us, and I swore I wouldn't offer it again, but, Jada, my pride can burn in hell because if I don't have you…there is no meaning. Pride won't keep me warm. Pride won't show me beauty. You are what I have been chasing all my life. This is the feeling. I thought I was dead inside, thought I could never, ever have this…and then there was you."

Jada looked at Alik, at the man who had changed her. At the man who was offering her healing. "I'm so sorry, Alik."

"What?" he asked, his voice choked.

"This is what I did to you, isn't it? I dragged you out of your safety, out of your comfort zone and I made you face everything that scared you the most."

"You did. But it needed to be done. Protecting myself…protecting myself from the pain of losing my mother would have kept me from truly connecting with my child. It would have kept me from connecting with you. From loving you."

"I was so arrogant to think I wasn't hiding, too. I was. I was hiding behind grief and excuses. I…I don't want to hide anymore. Alik, please, please forgive me. Please love me. Please tell me it's not too late."

He pulled her in, crushing his lips to hers, stealing her breath. When they parted, she was dizzy. "Of course it's not too late. In fact, I was planning on mounting a full-scale attack on your defenses."

She laughed. "As if you hadn't already!"

"I'm a strategist, remember? That's what they pay me for. And I had a plan to win you back."

"What was it?"

"I don't remember. I discarded it somewhere between the plane from Brussels to Attar, then I spent days in a hotel room, sulking and then I went and got this." He held his left hand up. There was a dark band tattooed around his ring finger.

"What is that?"

"My wedding ring. It doesn't come off, which, I thought might make for a nice line about why you actually have to stay married to me."

"Alik…"

She took his hand in hers and ran her finger over the band. "What does it say?" She looked up at him. "It's in Russian."

"Jada. And Leena. My family. I am committed to you, always."

"What if I would have told you I didn't want to be married to you?"

"Are you going to tell me that?"

"No."

"Then it's moot. But that was when I figured I would redraft a strategy and start working on ways to exploit your vulnerabilities."

"My vulnerabilities?"

"Yes. For one, I thought I could take you to the opera and get you alone in a private royal box."

"You are shameless."

"Always. But now…only for you. I have tasted every empty, meaningless pleasure life has to offer and I've come to the conclusion that those things are only there to distract us from the real meaning in life. A man can get lost in the fleeting things and forget to look for anything real. I am so thankful you brought something real into my life."

"Alik, I want you to marry me again," she said, thinking back to their wedding day. To the dress that she didn't like. To the lack of music. To her sadness. "And this time, I want to take your name. So we all have the same name. So I have your name."

"But what about…"

"The past is the past. I have good memories there. But now I'm not afraid to simply let memories be memories. Not anymore. I have too much ahead of me to keep looking back. You are my future. My heart. My love."

"And you have brought me love. For the first time, Jada. It's like seeing the sun, seeing color, when before there was only darkness. Only gray."

"Like waking up," she said, and she realized that it was true for her, too.

"Yes. Like that."

"I'm glad I woke up," she said. "Because this is so much better than dreaming."

"So much."

"So, will you marry me again?" she asked.

Alik looked at Jada, at his wife, at his heart. He had spent his life not feeling, not caring. And now that he did, he loved with all of himself. "No one ever loved me," he said. "And now, I have an embarrassment of riches. You and Leena? I am the luckiest man on earth. There are so many broken things in our lives and now…we get a chance to make something new. Something perfect."

She arched one brow and gave him an impish smile. "So, will you marry me, then?"

"Nothing could stop me."

"Don't go challenging fate, Alik."

"When I look at how things have played out, how I found Leena, how I found you, I think fate is on our side, don't you?"

"I think you're right."

EPILOGUE

J ADA ADJUSTED HER RED VEIL and held her arms out in front of her, examining the intricate designs that had been painted onto her skin during the henna ceremony the night before. Sayid's wife, Chloe, had helped with that and Jada was pleased that she'd found a friend in the other woman. Sayid was the closest thing Alik had to a brother. And now they were all family.

She could hear the music coming from the court-yard and her heart swelled, the smile that had been on her face since she'd woken up that morning spreading wider. She grabbed her bouquet from the dressing table and lifted her heavy skirt, adorned with gold fabric that caught fire when the mid-day Attari sun caught a hold of it. Bright, vibrant. Happy.

She ran down the stairs, her fingers skimming the stone balustrade. Two attendants opened the double doors for her, and she saw Alik, waiting for her at the head of the aisle, Leena in a red dress that matched Jada's, resting in his arms.

She nearly laughed, her heart taking flight. She looked up into the bleached sky and smiled. The heaviness that had been inside her for so long was gone, burned away by the sun, by the heat of Alik's love. She felt light again. She felt new.

Then she started to walk down the aisle. Toward her family, her husband. Her future.

Alik took her hand and she looked down at where they were joined, her hand small and dark in his. "I searched for this moment all my life," he said, his voice low. "What a gift to have finally reached it."

"I didn't realize I was searching for this moment," she said. "But I was. Out of grief came the most beautiful path. And it was taking me toward you, Alik."

"I'm so glad you followed it."

"So am I, Alik. So am I."

* * * * *